In The Name of the Lord

A Fictionalized Account of the Sexual Abuses of the Catholic Church

Dr. Robbie King

In the Name of the Lord

A Fictionalized Account of the Sexual Abuses of the Catholic Church

In the Name of the Lord

A Fictionalized Account of the Sexual Abuses of the Catholic Church

Dr. Robbie King

RK Enterprises Publishing

Kissimmee, Florida, United States of America

Copyright © 2024 by Dr. Robbie King and RK Enterprises Publishing, LLC.

In the Name of the Lord: A Fictionalized Account of the Sexual Abuses of the Catholic Church by Dr. Robbie King.

All rights reserved. No part of this publication may be reproduced, distributed, or transmitted in any form or by any means, including photocopying, recording or other electronic or mechanical methods, without the prior written permission of the publisher, except in the case of brief quotations embodied in critical reviews and certain other, non-commercial uses permitted by copyright law.

For permission, requests, write to the publisher, addressed "Attention: Permissions Coordinator" at the address below: Eaglewolf Wellness, LLC, 1680 Michigan Avenue, Suite 700-136, Miami Beach, FL 33139 United States of America. Or via email at drrobbieking00@gmail.com

Cover photograph by Pixabay and released under the free use license from pexels.com

Ordering Information: Quantity sales. Special discounts are available on quantity purchases by corporations, associations, and others. For details, contact the publisher at the address above.

Library of Congress Catalog Card Number: 1-9325181724

First Edition, First Printing.

ISBN: 979-8-882-76065-5

"Men never do evil so completely and cheerfully as when they do it from religious conviction."

- Blaise Pascal, French mathematician, physicist, inventor, philosopher and writer.

This book is dedicated to the thousands of victims of the sexual, psychological and additional physical abuses at the hands of the Catholic Church, the Legion of Christ, and Marcial Maciel.

In the Name of the Lord

A Fictionalized Account of the Sexual Abuses of the Catholic Church

Dr. Robbie King

Table of Contents

1. Author's Note 17
2. Author's Note 19
3. In the Name of the Lord 21

Author's Note

Dear Reader,

As you embark on this journey through the pages of my novel, you'll notice something distinct: it's written in screenplay format. This choice was not made lightly, and I'd like to share with you the reasons behind it.

I have always been fascinated by the immediacy and intensity that screenplays bring to storytelling. Inspired by Bill O'Reilly's innovative approach to history writing, I wanted to apply a similar method to fiction. By adopting this format, my aim is to plunge you directly into the heart of the action. This story is fast-paced, intense, and at times, brutally honest. The screenplay format, with its crisp dialogue and concise descriptions, captures this essence in a way that traditional prose simply couldn't.

I believe that this format makes the narrative not only more engaging but also more accessible. It allows for a rapid-paced storytelling style that is easy to digest, ensuring that you, the reader, are not just an observer but a part of the unfolding drama.

Some might argue that a play would suffice for such an approach, but I found that the theatrical format left too much to the imagination for this particular story. A screenplay, with its inherent 'in-your-face' nature, seemed the perfect medium to maintain the story's raw energy and immediacy.

So, as you turn these pages, imagine yourself not just reading a story, but watching it unfold before your very eyes. I hope this format enhances your experience and brings the characters and their tales to life in a vivid and impactful manner.

Thank you for joining me on this adventure. Your willingness to step into this unconventional format is greatly appreciated, and I hope you find the journey as thrilling as I found it in writing.

Sincerely,

Dr. Robbie King
Kissimmee, Florida, 2024

Introduction

It is no secret that the Catholic Church has a long and well-documented history of corruption, scandal, and abuse. These are not mere allegations but established facts that have marred the Church's legacy since its early days. The scandals have been varied and widespread, ranging from promiscuity at the highest levels, including several Popes, to bribery, and forming alliances with some of the most nefarious figures and regimes in history, such as Nazi Germany, Fascist Italy, and Spain, as well as the Spanish, French, and Portuguese Empires. The Church has been implicated in economic corruption, including the sale of indulgences that triggered the Protestant Reformation, usury, and predatory lending practices. It has exerted control over information, actively spreading anti-Semitism and hostility towards other religions, and has been responsible for the torture and extermination of millions in the name of religious conformity and imperial expansion.

The Church has sanctioned wars, granting special treatment to those who participated, and established educational systems that have led to the deaths of thousands. In many ways, the Catholic Church has been one of the most corrupt and criminal organizations in human history. However, as horrific as these deeds have been, they are merely the tip of the iceberg compared to the recent revelations of sexual abuse within the Church.

Sexual abuse within the Catholic Church is not an isolated phenomenon but a systemic issue that has occurred in every nation where the Church operates. It has permeated every level of the Church's hierarchy, from Popes to monks. Prominent figures such as Marcial Maciel, Cardinal Pell, and Pope John Paul II have either directly participated in these abuses, failed to adequately address them, or actively shielded and protected the abusers. The case of Pope John

Paul II's inaction against the repeated and systematic abuses committed by Marcial Maciel in Mexico is a stark example of this negligence.

These well-known but insufficiently addressed issues persist because the Catholic Church, due to its revered status, often operates above the law. But the time for silence and inaction is over. Too many lives have been destroyed, and too many people have been abused sexually, psychologically, and physically by this institution.

This book is another contribution to the growing chorus of voices demanding change and greater awareness. The story you are about to read is designed to denounce the sexual abuses committed by the Catholic Church upon young boys, a tragically common scenario. It is not based on a single tale but reflects the experiences of thousands, if not millions, of young boys whose innocence was shattered and bodies exploited by those who were supposed to be their spiritual guides.

This story is not for the faint of heart. It is brutal, but it is through this brutality and truth that we can expose the horrific realities of humanity and hope to effect change. Only by revealing what has truly happened can we begin to address the cover-ups and corruption that have protected the most corrupt organization in human history.

As you read this story, remember that it serves a purpose: to shed light on a subject that, even well into the 21st century, has been too often obscured to protect the guilty. It is a call to action, a plea for justice, and a demand for accountability.

IN THE NAME OF THE LORD

FADE IN:

INSERT - TITLE CARD:

"Massachusetts, 1985."

INT. CHURCH - NIGHT

FATHER CALLAHAN, 50'S, a priest with overwhelming moral toughness, is giving mass to dozens of boys, mostly between the ages of 10-13.

> FATHER CALLAHAN
> The Lord be with you...

> THE CONGREGATION
> And also with you...

> FATHER CALLAHAN
> May almighty God bless you, the Father, and the Son, and the Holy Spirit.

Father Callahan blesses the Congregation.

> THE CONGREGATION
> Amen...

> FATHER CALLAHAN
> Go in the peace of Christ...

> THE CONGREGATION
> Thanks be to God!

INT. CATHOLIC SCHOOL - CLASSROOM - DAY

In the classroom of an all-boys preppy catholic school, which is decorated with a large crucifix, a picture of Jesus, and a photograph of Father Callahan, a MALE TEACHER (also a priest), 50, is giving class to several boys, mostly aged from 12-13. The boys wear the school uniform.

> TEACHER
> Jesus says: "Turn the other cheek." And what does this mean, exactly? It means, love your enemies. Don't let them get the best of you... be the friends of your enemies. Evil, and grudge, have no place in life, as does vengeance. May your enemies do what they want, they can take your body, they can take your belongings, but they will never take your spirit.

In the back of the classroom sits JAKE, 12, a kid with a clean cut look mixed in with a certain rebellious attitude. Next to him sit two of his friends, BILLY, 12, and RONNIE, 12.

Jake has long hair, and his uniform is not as clean as would be expected from a student at this type of school. He is not paying attention to the teacher, and, although he pretends to be reading from the textbook, he is actually reading a satanic type, black metal article in a heavy metal magazine, which he is hiding behind the textbook.

The Teacher notices and looks at him with disapproval, and a certain anger.

                    TEACHER
        Do you understand what I'm saying
            kids? You are too young to
        understand what that means. But one
          day, you will face something that
          will inevitably push you towards
                 hate and vengeance.

The Teacher looks at Jake and discretely walks towards him.

                    TEACHER
        When that happens, don't fall into
           temptation... think like Christ.
         The evil ones will pay eventually.

The Teacher points at the painting of Jesus on the wall. The Teacher then walks towards Jake and RIPS the magazine from his hand. Jake is surprised.

                    TEACHER
              Isn't that right Jake?

The Teacher gets very irritated and looks at him with intensity. Just then,

THE BELL THAT ENDS THE CLASS RINGS.

The Boys get up from their seats and leave the classroom. The Teacher doesn't let Jake leave. He looks at the magazine with absolute disapproval.

                    TEACHER

> We'll see what the principal thinks
> about your satanic rock.

INT. CATHOLIC SCHOOL - PRINCIPAL'S OFFICE - DAY

Jake is standing in front of the SCHOOL PRINCIPAL, 54, a catholic priest with a profound conservative demeanor. He is holding Jake's magazine in his hand. The Teacher is standing next to him.

> PRINCIPAL
> How dare you come into this school,
> a school of God, with this garbage?

Jake remains silent, but he doesn't buy what the Principal is saying and rather takes it lightly.

The Principal shows him a picture where a black metal musician is playing the guitar. From his neck hangs an INVERTED CROSS.

> PRINCIPAL
> This is the symbol of Satan... You
> shouldn't be...

> JAKE
> (interrupting)
> They aren't Satanic!

The Principal gets very upset.

> PRINCIPAL
> Don't interrupt him Jake!

> JAKE

> (almost silently)
> Oh shit...

PRINCIPAL
Are you challenging me, Jake?

JAKE
Whatever... They aren't Satanic, it's all show... it's...

PRINCIPAL
(interrupting)
No Jake... When your elders are speaking you shut up! Understand? It's about respect! Don't disrespect me or this house! Do you want me to call your mother?

Jake doesn't care anymore.

PRINCIPAL
Now I realize that the magazine is the least of problems... you have an attitude problem, which needs to be adjusted. Or do you want to end up like your brother? Kicked out of ten schools? Without a future?

Jake is very upset.

JAKE
I don't care what you think! Better be my brother than a school principal like you!

The Teacher and the Principal are stunned.

INT. JAKE'S HOUSE - DINING ROOM - NIGHT

Inside a luxurious house, decorated with several religious type paintings, sits Jake, CHARLIE, 17 (Jake's Brother, a kid with an aura of absolute rebelliousness), and VALERIE, 35, (Jake's mother, a very attractive, and refined woman), having diner. Valerie looks upset.

                  VALERIE
Oh my God Jake! I can't believe it... that's exactly how your brother started.

Charlie gets upset by the comment but doesn't say anything.

                  JAKE
But mom, they're making such a big deal out of...

                  VALERIE
               (interrupting)
Jake that's exactly what the principal said... you can't keep your mouth shut... do you want to be suspended from the tournament? Do you want me to take you out of bass lessons? Huh? Do you want your grandfather to get upset?

                  JAKE
                No, but...

                  VALERIE
               (interrupting)
Then behave... if you want to play in the tournament you are going to

                    have to apologize to the Principal
                                and...

                              CHARLIE
                    But mom, you know damn well how
                    these guys are... they're a bunch
                                 off...

                              VALERIE
                            (interruting)
                    Charlie stay out of this! This
                         isn't your problem...

                              CHARLIE
                    Whatever... whatever the fuck
                               ever....

Charlie leaves the scene.

                               JAKE
                    Fine... I'll apologize to the
                              principal.

INT. SEMINAR - FATHER CALLAHAN'S OFFICE - DAY

Father Callahan is talking with Father O'SHEA, 31, a young priest with an aura of happiness and hard work.

                          FATHER CALLAHAN
                    Well, Father O'Shea, tell me, why
                    do you want to join us at the Order
                    of the Lord? Why do you want to be
                       a teacher here with us? Father
                    Kavanagh spoke very highly of you.

                          FATHER O'SHEA
                    I love Children, Father... it's my

27

>   reason for living. I love to help
>   them, talk to them, and, to a
>   certain extent, raise them. And
>   what better way to do this than
>   through God and through you? With
>   all the schools and children that
>   are under the Order of the Lord's
>   wing?

Father Callahan smiles.

>   FATHER CALLAHAN
>   Of course... and tell me, Father,
>   do you have any teaching
>   experience?

EXT. UNIVERSITY - STADIUM/FIELD - DAY

In a large football field, with many rows of seats, as well as bleachers, sit hundreds of people, they are facing a small stage that has been set up on one end of the field.

The field is full of boys and girls, all dressed in different school uniforms. Each team is sitting in a different part of the field with their respective squad. The parents of the kids are sitting on the bleachers around the stadium along with many different priests.

The leader of each different team carries a banner with the school they represent as well as the sport they are playing. Some read "basketball", others read "soccer", others "swimming", as well as many other sports. The teams are all in uniform.

Jake is sitting amongst a group of kids with a banner representing their school that reads "Forrest Hills School - Youth Basketball".

On the stage on the edge of the field sit several priests as well as a couple of people dressed in suits. On the center of the stage, a few feet behind the podium, sits Father Callahan. Everybody is looking at him.

Next to him sits FATHER FLANAGAN, 67, (his right-hand man), a man with a very intimidating look. Behind them stand SEXTON TAYLOR, 27, and SEXTON MARSHALL, 28, two physically imposing men whose job is to protect Father Callahan.

Valerie, Charlie, and PETER, 63, Valerie's Father, a very elegant man of obvious economic power, are sitting on the lower part of the bleachers looking at Jake, who seems to be ready to play ball. Charlie is dressed all in black and certainly looks out of place.

A MAN IN A SUIT, 56, the president of the ORDER OF THE LORD, is on the podium, speaking to the crowd, through the microphone.

>MAN IN SUIT
> This will been a wonderful tournament. Today we celebrate our thirtieth annual Order of the Lord Friendship Tournament. I want to thank you all for coming... Now, let me introduce you to the man who made this possible. Please welcome our father, our founder, and our leader, Father Paul Seamus

Callahan!

The entire congregation of people stand up from their seats and applaud Father Callahan. Jake looks at Father Callahan and smiles at him while he walks to the podium.

Father Callahan smiles at the crowd and brings his arms up. The applauding rises even more. He approaches the microphone.

>   FATHER CALLAHAN
> Good morning brothers and sisters
>   of the Order of the Lord...

The applauds dies off. Everyone smiles.

>   FATHER CALLAHAN
> First of all I would like to thank
>   you for coming today... I am very
>   happy that this tournament happened
>   and would like to thank everyone
>   who helped, sponsors, workers,
>   athletes, coaches, everyone...

The people look at him with awe.

>   FATHER CALLAHAN
>   Dozens of schools from around the
>   country and the world, have come
>   here to celebrate our day. These
>   means a lot to me, to us, and to
>   God.

People applaud and scream with joy.

>   FATHER CALLAHAN
> Our crusade has advanced so much...

> this fight for good and for God has had its fruits, and what we see today is a testament that our faith and love will always live on... but we still gave a lot of work to do. But everyday, the Order of the Lord gains more strength, and now, we are one of the most powerful catholic congregations in the world.

The people applaud again. The two Sextons look around, protecting him. Valerie and Peter revere Father Callahan, but Charlie does not at all.

FATHER CALLAHAN
This event has been very special for all of us, and it unites our cause even more, showing the competitive spirit that has characterized us for so long. God is smiling from above, and I wish I had a team so I could play with you all... I guess it will have to wait for next year.

Father Callahan smiles. The entire congregation laughs at his joke.

                    FATHER CALLAHAN
          I now officially open the thirtieth
          annual Order of the Lord friendship
            tournament. May we all play fair,
                  and may the best win!

Everyone stands up and applauds. Several fireworks are ignited.

INT. BASKETBALL GYM - DAY

A youth basketball game is taking place. The bleachers are filled with parents and supporters, and everyone is cheering. From a private bleacher, Father Callahan watches the game while he talks to a person of obvious economical power, who sits by his side.

Jake's team is one of the ones playing, and Jake is playing as a power forward and holds the "Captain" badge. The scoreboard reads "20-19", in favor of the other team. Not much time is left on the clock. Above the scoreboard there is a sign that reads "Boys Youth Basketball - Final".

Valerie, Peter, and Charlie are very excited while they watch the game from the stands.

Just then, Jake steals the ball from his own side and dribbles through the court, tricking many opposing players on the way.

Everyone in the stands starts screaming, including his family. Father Callahan watches cloooly.

Jake dribbles the ball and is about to do a lay up when an opposing player PUSHES HIM TO THE GROUND in a clear FOUL.

Valerie and Peter get angry.

                    PETER
                Foul! Foul!

                  CHARLIE
                Pig! Pig!

The people boo the foul. Jake stands up, and the ref signals a free throw. Jack takes the ball and stands on the free throw line.

                    PETER
                Common Jake!

                  VALERIE
           You can do it Jake!

Jake bounces the ball on the line. There is tension in the stands. Father Callahan looks at him closely.

Jake shoots the first throw and scores. The crowd cheers. He gets the ball again and shoots. The ball bounces on the ring, but falls into the net.

The people celebrate. Jake screams with Joy. The other team takes the ball but the game ends. The crowd celebrates.

EXT. UNIVERSITY - STADIUM/FIELD - DAY

It is almost nighttime, Father Callahan is standing on the podium on top of the stage, speaking to a large number of people, this time, closing the day.

Jake's team, with Jake as the leader, is sitting just in front of the podium. Valerie, Peter and Charlie are standing a few feet behind, next to many other parents. They watch Jake with a lot of pride.

> FATHER CALLAHAN
> (into microphone)
> This was quite a day... quite a tournament. We broke records in swimming, the female softball final went to extra innings, and we had an incredibly boys basketball finale. We had never had such a friendship tournament as we had today. Let us all walk tall, as no matter what the scores says, God knows, we are all winners!

Everyone, including Jake, applaud with vigor.

> FATHER CALLAHAN
> Now, to start the closing ceremony, I would like to award the first prize to the winners of the male youth basketball tournament... Forrest Hills Institute, champions of the friendship tournament for the third straight year! May the captain come up and receive the prize.

Everyone applauds. Jake stands up and smiles at his family. He approaches the podium. Father Callahan smiles at him, touches his head with affection, and gives him his diploma and trophy.

EXT. UNIVERSITY - STADIUM/FIELD - DAY

The Awards ceremony has ended. People are spread around the field. Jake is walking around with his trophy when he sees his family in the distance. He runs towards his mom. Valerie hugs him.

> VALERIE
> You did awesome Jake! Really.

> CHARLIE
> Yeah man... one hell of a free throw at the end...

> JAKE
> Thanks!

Jake sees his grandfather, Peter.

> PETER
> Come here champ!

His grandfather holds him and kisses him on the head.

> PETER
> One hell of a game! Now we're gonna go celebrate and for some the ice cream you like!

Jake smiles. He feels awesome. He looks at his mom. She smiles at him.

Just then, a masculine voice, is heard in the distance. It is the voice of LEONARD HANSEN, 37, a handsome, high-class man.

>LEONARD
>Valerie Hallenbeck!

Valerie gets frightened. She turns and sees Leonard. She immediately gets nervous, he looks a lot more handsome than she remembered. He walks towards her. Next him walks MANDY, 10, his daughter.

>VALERIE
>Leo...

>LEONARD
>My precious little Valerie... great to see you...

She's uneasy. They greet with a close hug and kiss.

>LEONARD
>I haven't seen you, in what? 15 years? Since College? We should meet up again some time.

Valerie SMILES and turns red.

>VALERIE
>Yeah... I'd love to...

INT. FANCY RESTAURANT - DAY

Valerie, Charlie, Peter and Jake are having dinner at a fancy restaurant.

>   PETER
>   I was just like you Jake... I
>   played ball all day, but I never
>   had the chance to win a game like
>   that...

>   CHARLIE
>   Yeah Jake... you were awesome...
>   and just wait until you play with
>   your band on stage... that's
>   something else... the best feeling
>   in the world.

>   VALERIE
>   It's almost the same right?

>   CHARLIE
>   Oh no... no way...

>   PETER
>   I wish I had played in the band...
>   I always wanted to play the
>   accordion but I was tone deaf... I
>   had an ear for artillery.

Jake laughs.

>   JAKE
>   An ear for what?

Peter laughs and grabs Jake's head with affection.

>   PETER
>   Nothing... so what? Do you wanna go

                    for ice cream after this?

                          JAKE
                 Yeah grandpa... thanks!

INT. JAKE'S HOUSE - DEN - DAY

It is a few days later. Valerie is sitting in a very luxurious, comfortable den, talking on the phone. She is dressed up and looks very attractive.

                         VALERIE
                      (into phone)
                Yeah girl... I'll be on my way to
                 get you in ten... let's go to the
                    bar we went to last time...

Jake walks into the room.

                          JAKE
                          Mom...

                         VALERIE
                      (into phone)
                       Yeah... bye...

She hangs up the phone and starts walking out of the room.

                          JAKE
                Mom I wanna go to the mall... can
                        you drive me?

                         VALERIE
                Um... Jake I can't, I'm in a
                hurry... Why don't you take a
                cab... There's money in my drawer.

                            38

                    JAKE
                   Okay...

                   VALERIE
                    By...

Valerie walks out of the room in a hurry.

INT. MALL - TOP FLOOR - DAY

Jake, Ronnie and Billy (his friends) are walking through the top floor of a mall. They are walking next to the railing, from which the other floors can be seen. Ronnie is holding a milk shake and Billy is holding an ice cream.

                    BILLY
       My parents didn't let me... I told
         them I wanted to drum lessons but
           they laughed at me... that if I
            wanted music, I should take up
          piano... and that's for girls...

                     JAKE
         Hell no... that's cool, you could
          be the keyboard player... and then
           we'll find someone that's not so
                gay to play the drums.

The three of them laugh. Just then, Ronnie spots something on the floor below.

                    RONNIE
            Wait... check that out...

They look over the railing and spot a GIRL, 14, who is walking by herself. She is dressed up, but looks a bit ridiculous.

                    JAKE
      Oh my God! Who does she think she
                    is?!

                    BILLY
       Isn't that Freddy's sister?

                  RONNIE
    Yeah! And just because of that...
     I'm gonna introduce her to a
       friend... Mr. Milk Shake.

Ronnie pulls his milk shake up. Billy and Jake laugh.

                  BILLY
     That'll be the day... do it... I
           dare you!

                  RONNIE
     Oh no... I couldn't... you do it
           Billy...

                  BILLY
          (interrupting)
          Yea sure...

                  JAKE
     I'll do it... you guys look like
           girls...

                  RONNIE
   Okay Mr. Big shot... let's see it.

Ronnie gives the milk shake to Jake. They stop at the railing, right ON TOP OF THE GIRL. They are laughing nervously. Jake doubts whether he should do it.

                    BILLY
               Common! Do it!

                    JAKE
             Okay... ready... set... go!

Jake pours the milk shake on the Girl, bathing her completely.

She looks around her. She's embarrassed. Milk Shake is dripping down her hair. She starts crying.

Billy, Ronnie and Jake laugh. She turns upwards and sees them. The three friends run away into a Music store.

INT. SOCIAL CLUB - CARD ROOM - NIGHT

In a poker table in the card room of a very luxurious social club sits Peter (Jake's grandfather), with other high profile businessmen. They are playing poker with large quantities of money, are smoking cigars, and drinking brandy.

                    PETER
             Yes... it was an amazing
          tournament. The best I've ever been
                      to.

A FRIEND OF HIS, 53, responds.

                    FRIEND 1
          I heard your grandson scored the
          winning points in the basketball
                     finals.

Peter feels proud.

                     PETER
           Yes, he did... played a hell of a
                    game too.

ANOTHER FRIEND, 60, speaks. The poker game
continues.

                    FRIEND 2
           And do you see a future for him
                   basketball?

Peter laughs.

                     PETER
          Are you kidding? Of course not... I
          already have one grandson stuck in
          no man's land... Jake's not going
          anywhere... After three daughters
          and only two male grandchildren,
          he's my last hope... I'm keeping
                   him with me...

                    FRIEND 1
          If its not him, then who's going to
          take care of the Hallenbeck family
                    business?

Everyone laughs. The Poker game continues.

INT. MALL - MUSIC STORE - DAY

Jake, Billy and Ronnie are walking inside the music store.

> JAKE
> Did you see her face? She never saw it coming!

> RONNIE
> But now you owe me a milk shake...

> JAKE
> (sarcastically)
> Yeah... sure...

Jake DISCRETELY pushes Ronnie, but Ronnie barely notices. The three of them continue watching the CD's on the rack. Most are pop albums.

> JAKE
> Nothing but crap in here... worst music in the world.

Ronnie picks up a CD from the rack. It is a pop album. He doesn't show it to his friends, but they notice.

> BILLY
> What do you have there?

> RONNIE
> Nothing...

> JAKE
> It's not one of your gay CD's, is it?

> RONNIE

                    Nope...

Jake rips it from his hand and shows it to
Billy.

                    BILLY
            As gay as it gets...

                    RONNIE
          Well I don't care what you guys
          think... I'm buying it. at least
          it's not Satanic, and at least I
          like it... you only listen to metal
               because of your brother...

Jake laughs.

                    JAKE
          Oh yeah? You're gonna buy it? With
                 what money?

                    RONNIE
               I've got my...

Ronnie puts his hand in his pocket but he
doesn't find his wallet and gets nervous.

                    RONNIE
            My wallet! Where is it?

Jake takes Ronnie's wallet out of his own
pocket.

                    JAKE
            Relax... I've got it...

Ronnie takes his wallet.

                    RONNIE
        What the hell is wrong with you?
          What are you, a thief now?

                    JAKE
        No! It's a just a trick a magician
          showed me... it's really easy.

                    BILLY
                Let's see it...

                    JAKE
        Look... all you need to do is...

Jake approaches Billy.

                    JAKE
        ...get near someone, distract
                    him...

Jake snaps his fingers next to Billy's ear.

                    JAKE
          ...and have quick hands...

Jake takes Billy's wallet.

                    JAKE
              It's that easy...

                    BILLY
        Wow... you're not coming into my
                house again...

They all laugh. Just then, Jake feels someone touching him in the shoulder. He turns and sees SECURITY GUARDS, the Milk Shake Girl, and the MOTHER OF THE MILK SHAKE GIRL, looking at him with anger.

Jake, Ronnie and Billy get very nervous.

INT. BAR - NIGHT

Inside a crowded lounge type bar, on a large table, sit Valerie, JEN, 32, a very attractive woman, and SUSY, 36, (equally attractive), and RICK, 26, a very handsome young man. They obviously like him, and are laughing, chatting, and drinking with him.

Valerie's phone is on the table. The music is at a very high volume.

                          JEN
           Common girl! You know I'm a decent
           girl! I wouldn't do that...

                       VALERIE
           We're all decent here, girl...

Everybody laughs. Just then, Valerie's expensive brick cell phone starts ringing. No one notices.

                       RICK
      But I've heard decent girls like
        everything... don't they?

They all laugh again. The cell phone keeps ringing and Valerie doesn't notice.

INT. MALL - SECURITY OFFICE - NIGHT

Jake is sitting on a bench inside the security office of the mall. The HEAD OF SECURITY, 36, is on the phone. Billy and Ronnie are not there.

                    HEAD OF SECURITY
          Your mom is not answering... Are
             you going to give me you
           grandfather's phone number or do
             you want to be here all night?

                         JAKE
          No, please no! Don't call the my
          grandpa, they already picked up my
              friends, just let me go! It was
            just one milk shake! I didn't no
                    anything bad!

                    HEAD OF SECURITY
          I am not going to argue... The fact
             is you attacked a young girl and
           caused a disturbance. You're lucky
           I'm not calling the cops. The rules
           make me call your parents, and you
             can't leave until they pick you
                         up.

                         JAKE
                        Fine...

INT. SOCIAL CLUB - CARD ROOM - NIGHT

The poker game has ended. Peter is standing in the same card room with a cigar in one hand

and a glass of brandy on the other, talking to a man who looks just as powerful as he does.

                    PETER
          Yes, you can count on it... I'd
           love to hear your proposition,
           construction is a very profitable
                   business.

His cell phone rings.

                    PETER
             (to man in front of him)
              Excuse me...

He answers the phone.

                    PETER
              Hello... What?

EXT. JAKE'S HOUSE - NIGHT

Valerie arrives at her house in her car. She has techno music at top volume and is definitely in party mode. She parks the car on the driveway.

INT. JAKE'S HOUSE - FOYER - NIGHT

Peter is standing in the foyer. He looks mad and impatient. He looks at his watch repeatedly. Jake is sitting on a chair next to him. He looks intimidated and worried.

Valerie walks into the house with a smile that quickly disappears once she sees her father.

INT. JAKE'S HOUSE - FOYER - NIGHT

Peter is screaming at Valerie, who is sitting in a chair. Jake is sitting next to her.

> VALERIE
> How dare you go out like a drunken slut... 'cause that's what you were doing, and not even know what's going on with the boy...

> VALERIE
> But dad, how was I supposed to know that Jake...?

> PETER
> (interrupting)
> That is your responsibility dammit! Or what, do you think I need the extra work?

Jake is worried.

> JAKE
> But grandpa I didn't do anything... I just...

Peter gets very angry.

> PETER
> Jake go to room! Now! When I talk, you shut up and listen! You got it?

Jake gets scared and walks towards his room.

> PETER
> This boy has a terrible problem with authority Valerie... he's been suspended from school, the thing

today at the mall, and right now he challenges me? What the hell is this... he's heading straight to Charlie's path...

VALERIE
Common dad... you're overreacting...

PETER
I'm overreacting!? We need to stop this now! This is my house, and here, we do what I say... you go it? What's going to be next? Drugs? Kicked out of school? Rehab? Like Charlie?

VALERIE
Then what? What do you want to do? Military school?

PETER
Something like that...

INT. JAKE'S HOUSE - JAKE'S ROOM - NIGHT

Jake is sitting in his room having a heated discussion with his mom. The room is decorated with basketball posters, a rock band poster, and a poster of the Hubble Space telescope picture detailing the millions and millions of stars and galaxies that exist in the universe.

JAKE
No mom! No way! I'm not going to any priest school! No way, I'm not going to be a priest.

                    VALERIE
        It's not a priest's school Jake,
        it's a seminary and a boarding
        school... and it's for the best...
            just for a little while...

                     JAKE
          What? No mom! No way! I'm not
                 leaving here!

                    VALERIE
        Jake, I know its hard... but you
        have no choice... your grandpa is
        very angry... you'll have a good
        time... besides, it's with Father
          Callahan, from the tournament.

                     JAKE
        I don't care... What about my band
        and my bass lessons? And what about
                   basketball?

                    VALERIE
        Look, you'll play there... and I
        promise, if you behave and change,
        you'll come back soon. In a few
            months... two or three...

                     JAKE
                    Oh no...

Jake is very upset.

INT. JAKE'S HOUSE - JAKE'S ROOM - NIGHT (LATER)

Jake is lying in his bed, playing the bass guitar, (he's pretty good at it) while he looks at the poster of the universe on the wall. He looks at it and relaxes a bit.

Knock on the door. Charlie comes in.

> CHARLIE
> I heard... you're leaving us...

Jake doesn't answer.

> CHARLIE
> Relax... at least you'll get out of here for a while...

> JAKE
> Yeah, it's really easy to say it right? I'm going to God knows where with kids I don't know... I won't play basketball...

He takes a basketball from the floor and starts playing with it.

> CHARLIE
> Relax... you'll be fine... I brought you something to take with you... you'll like it.

> JAKE
> What?

Charlie puts a PORNOGRAPHIC MAGAZINE and a MARIJUANA PIPE and a BAG with MARIJUANA on the bed.

> JAKE
> What's that?

Charlie takes the magazine.

>   CHARLIE
>   I think you know what this is...
>   and the other, well...

He takes the bag and the pipe.

>   CHARLIE
>   This is heaven... if one day you
>   feel bad... put this...

He shows him the actual marijuana.

>   CHARLIE
>   in the pipe... and smoke it...

>   JAKE
>   Smoke it?

>   CHARLIE
>   Sure... and paradise will come to
>   you...

>   JAKE
>   What?

>   CHARLIE
>   Just be careful who you share it
>   with... and enjoy...

EXT. BOARDING SCHOOL - FRONT YARD - DAY

Valerie's car is parked outside a big building situated inside a massive estate surrounded by a very big wall with only one entrance (an automatic gate).

Jake is sitting inside the car while Valerie is standing outside making him come out. Jake is dressed in a suit.

                  VALERIE
     Common Jake... get out of the car.

                    JAKE
                     No!

                  VALERIE
    Jake, we're already here... now get
    out... We made a deal and I'm going
      to stick to it... if you change
          you'll come back...

Jake finally gets out of the car. Valerie is also elegantly dressed. They start walking towards the entrance of the building. Suddenly, Valerie realizes something. She takes out a GOLDEN CRUCIFIX AND GOLDEN CHAIN from her purse.

                  VALERIE
    I almost forgot Jake... I wanna
           give you this.

She puts it around Jake's neck.

                  VALERIE
   It belonged to your grandma and she
   gave it to me when she died... it's
    over 100 years old and it's going
    to protect you when you need it. It
     looks great on you. Take care of
             it, okay?

                    JAKE

                              Okay.

Jake touches the cross and keeps walking
towards the entrance.

INT. BOARDING SCHOOL - PRIESTS' OFFICE -
WAITING ROOM - DAY

Jake and Valerie are sitting in the waiting
room. The place is decorated with many
different religious images, including a LARGE
PORTRAIT OF CHRIST.

FATHER RIVERS, 47, who's in charge of the
office, looks at them.

                         FATHER RIVERS
                    Father Callahan will be right
                    out...

                         VALERIE
                    Thank you...

INT. FATHER CALLAHAN'S OFFICE - DAY

Father Callahan gets up from his desk and
closes a drawer. Before he closes it, however,
we can clearly see a small LIQUID MEDICINE
CONTAINER and a XYRINGE. Father Callahan
stands up and leaves the room.

INT. BOARDING SCHOOL - PRIESTS' OFFICE -
WAITING ROOM - DAY

Valerie and Jake are sitting down when Father
Callahan comes out of his office. Jake is
surprised, he realizes this is the same man

who gave him the trophy at the friendship tournament.

> FATHER CALLAHAN
> Miss Hallenbeck?

> VALERIE
> Yes father... Valerie Hallenbeck... it's a pleasure.

She gets up from his seat and kisses Father Callahan's hand.

> VALERIE
> This is my son Jake, father.

Jake smiles at him.

> JAKE
> You're Father Callahan, from the friendship tournament.

Father Callahan smiles at him.

> FATHER CALLAHAN
> One and the same...

> VALERIE
> Jake played in the friendship tournament father...

> JAKE
> We won first place...

> FATHER CALLAHAN
> Of course, Forest Hills School... I remember, basketball.

Father Callahan takes out a lollipop from his jacket and gives it to Jake.

                FATHER CALLAHAN
                You want one?

Jake takes the lollipop.

                VALERIE
            What do you say, Jake?

                JAKE
                Thank you...

Father Callahan laughs with affection and touches Jake's head.

                FATHER CALLAHAN
       Please, come into my office mam...

Father Callahan points towards his office, which leads to the waiting room.

                FATHER CALLAHAN
                (to Jake)
          You wait here, little guy.

Valerie and Father Callahan walk into the office. She reveres him. Jake stays in the waiting room, looking at the images of Christ.

                FATHER RIVERS
       That's our Lord, Jesus Christ.

                JAKE
        Yes, I know who he is...

                FATHER RIVERS

> Everything here is done in his name...

INT. FATHER CALLAHAN'S OFFICE - DAY

Father Callahan is talking with Valerie.

> VALERIE
> We want him to change... he's a rebel child... and we want him back on track, Father.

> FATHER CALLAHAN
> Don't worry my child. I completely understand. You all relax... that's why we're here for... to remind society of the deeds of Christ and forge the souls of tomorrow, that is our vision here at the Order of the Lord. Jake is in excellent hands.

> VALERIE
> Oh, thank you so much Father.

> FATHER CALLAHAN
> You just need to remember that the times you come visit him must be very sporadic, and not too common, as he must learn to solve his own problems...

> VALERIE
> Of course, Father...

> FATHER CALLAHAN
> And please, we must keep the calls to him at a minimum. This place

will be his world, and he must not
remind him of the outside one...
and you are the only one allowed to
call him. And we don't allow email,
facebook, cell phones, or anything
of that sort. If their friends call
them or contact them, God knows
that all our effort could be lost
by a simple phone call or visit. Do
you understand?

                    VALERIE
Yes father... I'm grateful you are
so strict with that... Thank you so
much... is there anything else you
                     need?

                FATHER CALLAHAN
Well, we are in a vow of poverty
and only use what God gives us...
however, being that the tuition
only covers basic maintenance and
expenses, any kind of additional
help is always welcomed.

                    VALERIE
              Of course, Father...

Valerie takes out her checkbook, and before
writing down an amount, she hesitates.

                FATHER CALLAHAN
The amount doesn't matter. God is
fully aware of what is fair and
                    just...

EXT. BOARDING SCHOOL - FRONT YARD - DAY

Father Callahan, Jake, Father Rivers and Sexton Taylor (one of Father Callahan's bodyguards), are standing at the main entrance of the seminar watching as Valerie drives away.

Father Callahan is standing next to Jake and holds him with a certain disturbing affection. Jake and Father Callahan wave Valerie good bye. Father Callahan then turns towards Sexton Taylor.

> FATHER CALLAHAN
> Take Jake to the mess hall so he can meet his new schoolmates.

He turns towards Jake.

> FATHER CALLAHAN
> Jake, Sexton Taylor is will take you to have lunch and then one of our brothers will give you a tour of the school so you can get you know your knew home...

Jake nods. Sexton Taylor takes him.

> FATHER CALLAHAN
> I'll see you later Jake!

INT. BOARDING SCHOOL - MESS HALL - DAY

Jake walks into the mess hall with Sexton Taylor, who takes him to a large table with about forty children.

> SEXTON TAYLOR
> Sit here...

Jake sits between two kids, where an empty plate and silverware are standing. Sexton Taylor leaves. Jake looks around. The Mess Hall has about six tables for four children each, one for the priests, one for the sextons, and one round table for about ten children, who seem to be isolated.

While all the children on his table talk, Jake observes them. ANDY, 14, an overweight kid who is sitting beside him, looks at him.

                ANDY
            Are you new?

Jake looks at him with a certain affection.

                JAKE
       Yeah... I just got here...

                ANDY
     Do you know anyone else?

                JAKE
           Just you...

They both laugh slightly, causing a certain chemistry.

                ANDY
   That's how I started. But don't
  worry, you'll meet the rest soon.
  Where did they put you? With who do
           you sleep?

                JAKE
   I don't know... they haven't told

>   me...

Jake gets worried.

>   ANDY
>   Don't worry... they arrange us by
>   tables... so if you're not in my
>   room you'll be in the one next to
>   me... we're always together. We
>   have big rooms.

Jake looks at the kids at the round table.

>   JAKE
>   All of us? What about them? Why do
>   they have a different table?

Andy looks at them with a certain pity.

>   ANDY
>   They are special...

>   JAKE
>   Why?

>   ANDY
>   You don't wanna know...

Jake looks at them. Those kids aren't even talking. They are quiet and relaxed. Jake accepts what Andy has told them.

>   JAKE
>   Whatever...

The Waiters start serving the food. They start on Jake's table. Jake anxiously waits for her food. It is rice and meatballs.

                    ANDY
              Yummy... meatballs.

Andy immediately begins eating. Jake looks at
the food with apathy but starts eating. Just
then, on the other side of the table, ALBERT,
13, a kid who looks arrogant and pedant,
throws a meatball at ANDY'S FACE. Andy looks
at him in shock. So does Jake.

                   ALBERT
              Eat up piggy!

Albert and his friends laugh. Jake looks at
him with disbelief. Andy eats on.

INT. BOARDING SCHOOL - MESS HALL - DAY (LATER)

Everyone is leaving the mess hall. Jake walks
next to Andy when Father O'Shea stops him.

                FATHER O'SHEA
              Are you Jake?

Jake looks paranoid.

                    JAKE
              How do you know that?

                FATHER O'SHEA
         Easy... Andy's friends are always
            hiding something... right Andy?

Andy and Jake look at him with a certain fear.

                FATHER O'SHEA
           Relax... you're not wearing the

>   school uniform and they told me to
>   give a school tour to the new
>   boy...

                         JAKE
                    Yeah... that's me...

                     FATHER O'SHEA
                    Great... let's go...

Jake turns towards Andy.

                         JAKE
                    See you later.

                     FATHER O'SHEA
               Take it easy Andy... oh, by the
               way... I brought you something...

Father O'Shea takes out some candy from his
pocket and gives it to Andy. Andy smiles.

                         ANDY
                       Thanks!

INT. BOARDING SCHOOL - CHAPEL - DAY

Jake and Father O'Shea are walking through the
chapel.

                     FATHER O'SHEA
               This is the chapel Jake... here you
                can come to prey whenever you
               want... and here we come to mass on
                         Sundays.

                         JAKE
                    (apathetically)

                    Okay... cool.

                    FATHER O'SHEA
            You wanna see the giant bell Jake?

                         JAKE
              I don't really care... whatever.

                    FATHER O'SHEA
                         Why?

                         JAKE
            Because I'm only going to be here
            for a while... Only for a couple of
            months... I'm not going to be a
            priest. As soon as I can I'm
            leaving. My mom only sent me here
            so I could change...

                    FATHER O'SHEA
            Oh no Jake... I think your mom sent
            you here to learn something... How
            do you know you're not going to be
            a priest? How do you know you don't
            want to spend the rest of your life
                    serving God?

                         JAKE
            Boooring... I'm going to be a bass
            player for a rock band or a
            professional basketball player.

Father O'Shea laughs amiably.

                    FATHER O'SHEA
            Well, that's something to look up
            to... the important thing is to do
            what you like... I didn't know I

> was going to dedicate my life to
> God... but one day it struck me...
> the important thing is to give it
> all you got.... if you wanna be a
> musician be the best, if you wanna
> be a star athlete, give it your
> best... that's the important thing.
> Be strong... don't think about
> what's going on at home... live for
> the moment...

Father O'Shea leans on a table on the ALTAR and accidentally pushes the incense to the floor. The incense spills all over and causes a huge thud.

Jake starts laughing. Father O'Shea laughs too; they like each other.

EXT. BOARDING SCHOOL - YARD - DAY

Jake and Father O'Shea are walking through a gigantic yard next to the wall of the school. The sun is about to set.

> FATHER O'SHEA
> You are going to be assigned a
> chore to help our community at the
> school... everybody has one.
> Sometimes you're going to wash
> clothes, sometimes you're going to
> water the yard, clean the windows.

Jake makes a face of "I'm not doing it". Father O'Shea sees it.

> FATHER O'SHEA
> But don't see it as a burden...

> you're gonna have fun... it's part
> of the experience...

> JAKE
> Yeah, sure...

They keep walking for several feet until they spot something that looks like a dead animal lying on the ground. They look at it in detail and see that it is an injured hawk, with a broken wing. The hawk is trying to get up, but it can't.

> JAKE
> Look, the birdie's hurt.

> FATHER O'SHEA
> Let me see...

He leans down to grab it but the hawk doesn't let him.

> FATHER O'SHEA
> It's a hawk..

> JAKE
> What happened to him?

> FATHER O'SHEA
> I don't know... I think his wing is
> broken...

> JAKE
> And what do we do? Is he going to
> die?

> FATHER O'SHEA
> No... we just have to take care of

him until he gets better...

                    JAKE
            Let's get some help...

                 FATHER O'SHEA
            No, no, no Jake... they're not
            going to let us keep him... we'll
            take care of him, it'll be our own
            little secret. Help me carry him.

Father O'Shea takes off his stole and wraps the hawk in it.

EXT. BOARDING SCHOOL - MAIN BUILDING - ROOF - DAY

Father O'Shea and Jake put the hawk in an improvised cage. Jake fills a small glass with water and puts some raw meat on a small bowl.

                 FATHER O'SHEA
            We're going to keep him here until
            he gets better, okay? We'll take
            turns in visiting him and feeding
            him... and in a few weeks he'll get
            better and we'll let him go.

                    JAKE
            Okay... I like that...

                 FATHER O'SHEA
            What are you going to name him
                    Jake?

                    JAKE
            I don't know...

                    FATHER O'SHEA
                 How about Phoenix?

                        JAKE
                      I like it...

He looks at the hawk.

                        JAKE
                      Phoenix...

INT. BOARDING SCHOOL - MAIN BUILDING - HALLWAY - DAY

Jake and Father O'Shea are walking in the hallway when, suddenly, Sexton Taylor runs into them.

                    SEXTON TAYLOR
              Where were you? We were looking for
                         you...

                    FATHER O'SHEA
               I was giving Jake a tour of the
               school... just like Father Callahan
                      instructed me.

                    SEXTON TAYLOR
                       (to Jake)
              Well then, let's go... it's getting
                          late.

                        JAKE
                   (to Father O'Shea)
                    See you later...

69

Sexton Taylor puts his hand on Jake's back and takes him away. Father O'Shea blinks his eye at Jake.

Jake and Sexton Taylor continue walking through the hallway when they spot a YOUNG BOY, 10, who is walking out of Father Callahan's office. The Young Boy looks depressed and down, and looks at the floor while he walks.

Father Callahan is standing at the door that leads to his office while he looks at the boy with a disturbing look.

              FATHER CALLAHAN
         Good night, Phillip.

Father Callahan then turns towards Jake and Sexton Taylor while they walk through the corridor. Father Callahan smiles at Jake and then walks back into his office. Sexton Taylor and Jake continue walking for several feet until the reach a door.

              SEXTON TAYLOR
    This is your room. Your bed is the
     empty one... you can't leave the
      room until morning... is that
                 clear?

                  JAKE
                 Yes...

Sexton Taylor pushes him into the room and closes the door.

INT. BOARDING SCHOOL - JAKE'S ROOM - NIGHT

Jake lies down on the only empty bed. The place is completely dark and all the other kids are asleep. Jake's bed is next to the window.

Jake sits down in his bed, looks beneath it and sees that his suitcase is right there. He lies down in the bed and looks out the window. The night sky is lit bright and has a large similarity to Jake's poster of the Hubble space telescope picture in his room at home.

Jake looks at the cosmos for several seconds and relaxes. He then moves his hand and touches his suitcases. He takes out the MARIHUANA PIPE and looks at it with curiosity.

He then puts the pipe away and grabs the necklace his mother gave him and keeps looking at the cosmos.

INT. JAKE'S HOUSE - DINING ROOM - NIGHT

Charlie, Valerie and Peter are having dinner. There is a feeling of uneasiness at the table.

               VALERIE
    It was hard to leave him... poor
                Jake.

                PETER
    Don't even think about it... I know
    where you're getting at... we're
     all sad but Jake is staying
            there...

               VALERIE
    I wasn't saying that... I was

                    just...

                    PETER
                (interrupting)
          Don't even think about... find
          yourself something to do or
          whatever... forget him for now...

                    CHARLIE
          Well, what's the shame in a visit
          once in a while? He's not in
                    jail...

                    PETER
          Stay out of this Charles! Jake is
              fine... leave him be...

                    CHARLIE
          Easier said than done, right?

Peter gets upset.

                    PETER
          Charles, why don't you leave?

                    CHARLIE
          I'm not going to give you the
                   pleasure...

They keep dining. The tension is overwhelming.

EXT. BOARDING SCHOOL - YARD AREA - DAY

Jake and several other kids are playing a basketball game in a cement basketball court next to the large grass yard. The sun is shining with total intensity. FATHER VICK, 34, is supervising the children.

Jake is dribbling the ball with a lot of skill through the court. The kids follow him and the other team tries to take the ball away, but they can't.

Jake dribbles the ball until he reaches the other basket and tries to do a lay up to score. Before he does so, however, Albert, the kid who threw the meatballs at Andrew at the mess hall, pushes him. Jake falls to the ground and I unable to shoot.

Jake looks at him with aggression, but contains himself. The kids yell "free throw, free throw", repeatedly. Jake stands up and grabs the ball.

He stands in the free throw line. The kids put themselves around him, waiting for him to shoot. He shoots the ball but with too much force. The ball flies away from the court and doesn't even hit the board where the basket is. Albert laughs at him.

                    ALBERT
            Go get it, loser!

Jake looks at him with impotence, and he has no choice but to go get the ball. The ball, however, bounced away to a great distance and into a sort of ditch.

                    ALBERT
     Oh... and you're gonna have to go
         get it in the tunnels.

Jake then looks at Albert with a certain impotence and starts running towards the tunnels. As he runs, however, he approaches Albert and HITS HIM with his elbow. Albert falls to the ground. He is very angry. Jake runs to get the ball.

                    ALBERT
          Yeah, you better walk away! 'Cause
                   I'll kill you!

Jake laughs at Albert.

                    JAKE
                   Sucker!

EXT. BOARDING SCHOOL - AREA NEAR THE TUNNELS - DAY

Jake is walking through the yard en route to a large ditch/well that leads to an underground tunnel.

                    JAKE
            Tunnels? Which Tunnels?

Jake looks at the ditch and walks towards it. He stands on the edge. It is very deep. He doesn't know whether to jump in. He looks back at the other kids, who are yelling at him to get in.

He is about to jump into the tunnel when suddenly, Sexton Taylor grabs him from behind and stops him.

                 SEXTON TAYLOR
          Where do you think you're going?

Those tunnels are forbidden! No one can go in there!

                JAKE
But I was just going to get the ball...

           SEXTON TAYLOR
That ball is lost... those tunnels are very dangerous... you should know that!

                JAKE
But...

           SEXTON TAYLOR
            (interrupting)
But nothing... let's go... I'm taking you to father Callahan...

                JAKE
But why?

INT. BOARDING SCHOOL - PRIESTS' OFFICE - WAITING ROOM - DAY

Jake is nervously waiting in the waiting room. He is looking at the painting of Christ on the wall when Sexton Taylor comes out of Father Callahan's Office.

Father Callahan looks at Jake with a disturbing look.

           FATHER CALLAHAN
Jake... step into my office.

Jake gets very nervous.

INT. BOARDING SCHOOL - FATHER CALLAHAN'S OFFICE - DAY

Father Callahan is sitting at his desk, talking with Jake, who looks nervous. Jake is sitting in a chair in front of the desk.

              FATHER CALLAHAN
    Sexton Taylor told me you were
    trying to get into the underground
                  tunnels.

                    JAKE
                Yes, but...

              FATHER CALLAHAN
               (interrupting)
    Those tunnels are very dangerous
    Jake... they are flooded, and a boy
    your age drowned there a few years
    ago and God would not want that to
    happen to you... What would we do
           without you Jake?

                    JAKE
      But I just lost my ball...

Father Callahan laughs slightly.

              FATHER CALLAHAN
    Ball? You were going to get your
    ball? No Jake, don't ever do that
       again... it's not worth it...

Father Callahan stands up and walks towards a closet.

                    FATHER CALLAHAN
              If you ever lose a ball again, you
                       let me know...

Father Callahan opens the closet, where there
are dozens of different types of balls as well
as toys.

                    FATHER CALLAHAN
              ...and I'll give you another one...

Father Callahan grabs a ball and gives it to
Jake.

INT. BUILDING - NEWSPAPER OFFICE - OFFICE OF
MR. HARPER - DAY

ALVIN HARPER, 34, a reporter and journalist,
is sitting at his desk inside a very nice
office. On the wall hang several awards and
titles from different newspapers as well as
cutouts from important events in history. A
large pile of newspapers is also stacked up
against the wall.

Harper is on the phone. He talks with passion.

                         HARPER
              Never! I said never! I bought that
              story! He came to me and told me he
              wanted me to tell his story! Not
                         you! Me...

Harper laughs.

                         HARPER
              If you want it... It'll be in print
                         next week.

He hangs up the phone.

> HARPER
> Jackass...

Someone knocks on the door. MR. MARTIN, 54, Harper's Boss, comes in.

> MR. MARTIN
> We have a problem Alvin... Kelvin quit...

> HARPER
> (sarcastically)
> Oh... that's a load off...

> MR. MARTIN
> We have no one else to do the Father Callahan story...

> HARPER
> Don't even think about it! I'm not doing it... I'm a serious journalist, I'm not going to advertise Father Callahan... find someone else...

> MR. MARTIN
> Do it... Trust me, it's worth it... no one has ever done a real story one him... there could be a lot of murky water there... you might get something interesting... and he's already granted two interviews...

Harper laughs.

HARPER
         Why don't you just tell me the
          truth... I know he gave us money
             for the interview... but
            whatever... I'll do it... now
            leave, I got some real work to
                         do...

Mr. Martin is about to leave but before exiting he turns towards Harper.

                  MR. MARTIN
           Just don't fuck it up will you?

EXT. BOARDING SCHOOL - YARD - DAY

In one of the boarding school's yards (located next to a very high wall), stand several kids congregated around a very tall TREE (much taller than the wall) located exactly next to the wall. They watch as Albert, the boy who committed the foul against Jake earlier, is climbing the tall tree. The boys motivate him to continue climbing.

From a moderate distance, Jake and Andrew observe everything. THERE IS NOT FATHER GUARDING THEM.

Albert keeps climbing. Just then, FATHER HARRIS, 30, arrives at the scene and sees what they are doing.

                 FATHER HARRIS
          What are you doing? Albert get down
                from there now!

Albert looks at Father Harris in fear.

> FATHER HARRIS
> Get down from there now or...

Albert lets go and falls directly to the ground. He falls on his arm and starts crying.

> ALBERT
> My arm! My arm!

Father Harris, Jake and the rest of the boys approach him.

> FATHER HARRIS
> I told you Albert! I told you! No one can climb that tree! Now look what you did!

Jake looks at the tree and sees that is has a carved inscription. "Commemorative Tree - Creation of the Order of the Lord. 1970 - Present."

Albert continues moaning. Jake approaches him.

> JAKE
> We have to take him to the nurse.

> FATHER HARRIS
> Pick him up...

Jake and Andrew help Albert up and start to take him to the nurse. Father Harris does nothing. He simply observes.

EXT. BOARDING SCHOOL - OUTSIDE NURSE'S OFFICE - DAY

Jake and Andrew help Albert as he walks towards a door with a RED CROSS. He keeps crying. Jake knocks on the Nurse's door. A MALE NURSE, 35, comes out of the office and helps Albert walk in.

                    ALBERT
                   (amiably)
            (to Jake and Andrew)
                   Thanks...

The Nurse closes the door. Jake and Andrew sit down outside the office. He turns to his side and sees Father Callahan, Father Vick, Sexton Taylor, Father O'Shea and Father Flanagan, walking together.

Father Callahan sees Jake sitting outside the Nurse's office and approaches him. Father O'Shea sees him as well.

                FATHER O'SHEA
                   Hi Jake...

                    JAKE
                    Hi...

              FATHER CALLAHAN
    Jake, what are you doing here? Why
    aren't you playing basketball with
      the other boys? Don't you have
                recess now?

Father Callahan looks at his watch.

              FATHER CALLAHAN
    You didn't lose another ball, did
                    you?

Jake laughs. Father O'Shea looks at Jake with affection. But given that Father Callahan is present, he dares not open his mouth.

                JAKE
No, it's just that Albert hurt his arm and I brought him to the nurse.

           FATHER CALLAHAN
Oh, excellent Jake... I'm glad you help your classmates... that's the way it must be... Jesus always helps those who help others... looks like you are doing great Jake... How is everything? You do seem more relaxed than before...

                JAKE
Yes but, I want to see my mom...

Father O'Shea breaks the silence.

            FATHER O'SHEA
No Jake... remember what we talked about? You need to be strong...

Everyone turns towards Father O'Shea.

            FATHER O'SHEA
Why don't you wait? You've only been here two weeks...

           FATHER CALLAHAN
Well, if the boy wants to see his mom who's to blame him? This is completely normal... I feel the same if I were you... don't worry

               Jake, I will bring your mom soon.

Jake turns towards Father Callahan with
admiration and smiles at him. Father O'Shea
sees this and looks at Jake with sadness. He
knows he's lost him. Father Callahan has beat
him.

                    FATHER CALLAHAN
                 See you later, Jake...

They walk away. Jake looks at Father Callahan
with admiration.

EXT. OUTSIDE RELIGIOUS SCHOOL - STREE - DAY

A large, LUXURY CAR parks outside the main
door of an all-girls religious institution. It
is located in an upper-class neighborhood.

Sexton Taylor gets out of the car from the co-
pilot seat. He is dressed in a much more formal
manner. He opens the back door. Father
Callahan and Father Flanagan climb out of the
car. They walk towards the entrance of the
school.

EXT. RELIGIOUS SCHOOL - MAIN YARD - DAY

Father Callahan is talking with TWO NUNS, 45,
and 52, while they walk through the main yard
of the school. With them walks Father
Flanagan, and Sexton Taylor walks behind them.

The school is a nice one, but it is not very
big.

                       NUN 1

We have made a lot of progress
Father... every year we have more
female pupils and we hope to
increase our graduates by 100% in
five years. We will be expanding
the facilities of the school very
soon.

FATHER CALLAHAN
Perfect, don't forget to let me
know so that I can send necessary
help... Oh, incidentally, why
didn't the boys school have any
team represent them at the
friendship tournament this year?

NUN 2
Well, the new projects have
obligated us to cut funds from
athletic activities...

FATHER CALLAHAN
Please sister, when something like
that happens let me know... don't
let money be a barrier with the
education of our children.

Father Callahan turns towards Father Flanagan.

FATHER CALLAHAN
Father Flanagan, please hand me the
checkbook.

Father Flanagan gives him the checkbook.
Father Callahan signs a check for a LARGE SUM.

FATHER CALLAHAN
I hope this will be enough. If it

>   is not let me know so I can send
>   more... but don't let that happen
>   again...

                         NUN 1
               Of course not, Father... thank
                          you...

                         NUN 2
             Father would you like to see the
             girls right now? So they can thank
             you personally. The boys are out on
              a goodwill mission, but the girls
                    would love to see you...

Father Callahan smiles.

INT. RELIGIOUS SCHOOL - CLASSROOM - DAY

About 20 senior girls (aged between 17-18), dressed in their school uniforms, are taking class with a PROFESSOR, 36, when the two nuns, Father Callahan, Father Flanagan, and Sexton Taylor walk into the classroom.

The girls immediately recognize Father Callahan. The entire class shuts up. The girls look at him with admiration. They smile at him.

                         NUN 1
              These are our seniors father. They
              will be the next to graduate... the
                next ones to jump into the real
                          world.

                    FATHER CALLAHAN
              Congratulations all of you... may

> God be with you... and I hope you
> continue the way we showed you and
> spread the word of our Lord.

The girls look at him with total admiration. Father Flanagan observes everything quietly.

> NUN 2
> Would you like to take a picture
> with the girls Father?

INT. RELIGIOUS SCHOOL - CLASSROOM - DAY (LATER)

The girls, the Nuns and a few other teachers are congregated as though a picture was going to be taken. Smack in the middle of them, ready for the photograph, sits Father Callahan.

Sexton Taylor focuses the camera on the girls and Father Callahan. Father Flanagan observes everything from behind.

> SEXTON TAYLOR
> Perfect... that's great. Everyone
> smile...

The girls smile even more.

> SEXTON TAYLOR
> Perfect... say cheese... Smile! You
> are with Father Callahan!...

The girls smile even more. Sexton Taylor takes the photograph.

INT. BOARDING SCHOOL - OFFICE - WAITING ROOM - DAY

Father Callahan, Father O'Shea, Father Flanagan, Sexton Taylor, Sexton Marshall, several other priests and several REPORTERS, CREW, and CAMERAMEN, as well as Reporter Harper, are preparing themselves for an interview with Father Callahan.

Some of the crew is putting a microphone on Father Callahan and putting on a light make up. Meanwhile, Father Flanagan speaks to Reporter Harper.

>FATHER FLANAGAN
>(Irish accent)
>Just as we agreed over the telephone, Mr. Harper. The interview will be divided into two separate dates. Part 1, and Part 2... I know you want to ask many questions, but you will only ask the ones I sent you earlier. No others... and no sneaky photographs... you have to ask us before taking any pictures...

>Mr. Harper gets a bit upset.

>HARPER
>I will ask what I deem convenient... and you told me I could take all the pictures I needed... if not, why did...

>FATHER FLANAGAN
>(interrupting)
>Look Mr. Harper... those are the terms of the interview... take

>   them, or leave them... I don't
>   think you would want to waste the
>   time it took you to get here...
>   better do what we agreed.

Mr. Harper is upset, but has no choice.

INT. BOARDING SCHOOL - HALLWAY - DAY

Mr. Harper, Father Flanagan, Sexton Taylor, Sexton Marshall, two cameramen (without cameras) and several other priests, are following Father Callahan while he walks down the hallway. Mr. Harper holds a tape recorder while he follows Father Callahan.

>   HARPER
>   Tell us Father... as leader of the
>   Order of the Lord, possibly the
>   largest christian organization in
>   the world, what are your
>   expectations for this year?
>
>   FATHER CALLAHAN
>   Well, we are always looking for
>   more souls to join us in our
>   cause... through Christ we seek to
>   give a purpose to the lives of so
>   many people... we are not content
>   with only being the fastest growing
>   catholic congregation in the
>   world... we need to keep spreading
>   the word...
>
>   HARPER
>   Father... a recent article
>   stipulated that you, as an
>   organization, receive an amount

>   close to 700 million dollars a year
>   from people around the world. Is
>   this true? How do you use this
>   money to fulfill your mission?

Father Callahan is surprised by the question. He turns towards Father Flanagan, who seems angry at Reporter Harper. Father Callahan is cornered, but he keeps answering.

>   FATHER CALLAHAN
>   For us, money is not valuable...
>   the real value and real investment
>   is in the souls of our followers.

Harper realizes Father Callahan is evading his question.

>   HARPER
>   But 700 million is not spare
>   change... what exactly do you do
>   with it?

Father Callahan gets a bit angry and upset, but doesn't show it.

>   FATHER CALLAHAN
>   It's not an easy task, surely...
>   but what we get in exchange from
>   these young souls is priceless...
>   And I will prove it to you... let's
>   go into a classroom.

They walk several feet and stop at a door. Sexton Marshall opens it for them. Father Callahan walks in, followed by Harper and the rest of the people. A CAMERAMAN, 40, takes out his camera and is about to discretely take a picture of Father Callahan when Sexton Taylor GRABS THE CAMERA WITH VIOLENCE AND PUSHES IT DOWN.

> SEXTON TAYLOR
> We said no sneaky pictures!

The Cameraman gets frightened. No one around sees the incident, as they are already in the classroom.

INT. BOARDING SCHOOL - CLASSROOM - DAY

Father Callahan, Father Flanagan, Father O'Shea, Mr. Harper and a few more are standing inside a classroom full of young boys. Jake is sitting in the middle, next to Andrew. Mr. Harper is standing next to Father Callahan.

Father O'Shea blinks his eye towards Jake, and Jake smiles at him.

> FATHER CALLAHAN
> This what I was talking about...
> these are our boys, those who give
> us hope for the future... these are
> the souls of tomorrow.

Jake looks at them.

> HARPER
> And are all these boys studying to
> become priests? To serve the
> church? Just as you have, Father
> Callahan?

Father Flanagan looks at Mr. Harper with toughness.

                    FATHER CALLAHAN
          Well we want them to be involved in
            the church as much as they can... I
            am sure these lives will be linked
              to the church no matter what
                   happens in the future...

Father Callahan turns towards a BOY, 13.

                    FATHER CALLAHAN
            Let's see... you... Eddie... how
                   will you serve God?

The Boy gets a bit intimidated, but
nonetheless responds.

                         BOY 1
                I want to be an architect...

                    FATHER CALLAHAN
            And wouldn't you want to build a
                         church?

The Boy is not so convinced about the
question. But still answers.

                         BOY 1
                  Yes, of course I would...

                    FATHER CALLAHAN
                       (to Harper)
                   See what I mean?

He turns towards Jake.

                    FATHER CALLAHAN
            And you, Jacob? What do you want to

                    be?

                   JAKE
         Well, I like music father...

              FATHER CALLAHAN
         Wonderful... sacred music is one of
         a kind... there's also choir music,
         and religious organ pieces... what
                   do you like?

Jake responds with a lot of emotion.

                   JAKE
            I like hard rock!...

All the boys laugh. Father O'Shea smiles and
Harper laughs slightly. Father Callahan is a
bit ashamed and smiles falsely, but he is
obviously angry. Father Flanagan looks at
Jake with an intense look.

              FATHER CALLAHAN
         Well... after this brief pause,
            please accompany me to the
         chapel... we have just remodeled
                     it...

EXT. BOARDING SCHOOL - BUILDING - ROOF - DAY

It is the afternoon. Jake is sitting on the
roof looking at the sunset while he guards
Phoenix, who is sitting on her cage.

                   JAKE
         Hi Phoenix... How are you doing
                   birdie?

Jake takes out some leftover bread from his pockets and gives them to the bird. The bird gradually eats the bread and then drinks some water from his plate. Jake looks at the animal with fondness until he hears a noise. He turns and sees that it is Andy, who is spying on him.

                    ANDY
        What are you doing? Are you crazy?

                    JAKE
        I am just taking care of him until
                he gets better...

                    ANDY
        If I were you I'd let him go... if
            they catch you you're dead...

                    JAKE
        Nobody is going to catch me okay?
        If they get me it's because of
        you... so shut up or I'll tell them
                you were in on it.

In the distance, the voice of the JANITOR, 58, can be heard.

                 JANITOR (O.S.)
              Hey who's there?

Jake and Andy turn and see the Janitor. They are very alarmed. Andrew starts running away.

                   JANITOR
            Hey! Where you going?!

Andy runs down the stairs and disappears. Jake doesn't know whether to run or stay. Just as he is about to take off, the Janitor stops him.

                    JANITOR
                      Stop!

Jake stops. The Janitor walks towards him.

                    JANITOR
       ...the roof is forbidden... you
              can't be here...

                      JAKE
                      but...

The Janitor walks towards the hawk's cage and sees that the bird is inside it.

                    JANITOR
            Oh... it's a bird...

                      JAKE
         His name is Phoenix...

The Janitor is amiably surprised by Jake's confidence. He laughs slightly in a nice manner.

                    JANITOR
     Phoenix? And why do you have him
                 here?

                      JAKE
     He's hurt... I'm only going to take
       care of him until he's fine...
         please don't tell on me...

The Janitor smiles.

                    JANITOR
          Alright... I won't... but on one
           condition... you need to let me
                  visit him too.

The Janitor smiles at Jake. Jake smiles at him.

                     JAKE
                   Thanks...

INT. BOARDING SCHOOL - JAKE'S ROOM - NIGHT

Jake and the rest of the boys are playing around, pillow fighting, jumping in the bed, pushing themselves around. Jake is playing pillow fights. Just then, Sexton Taylor walks into the room unnanounced.

                 SEXTON TAYLOR
          Go to sleep... you have one minute!

At that moment all the kids lie down. Sexton Taylor turns off the lights.

                 SEXTON TAYLOR
                  Good night...

He closes the door and leaves. In an instant, everybody shuts up and drifts into sleep. Jake shuts up and quietly observes the stars through the window. He then makes sure everyone is asleep and looks in his suitcase.

He takes out the PIPE and the MARIHUANA BAG. He looks at them in detail but then doubts and puts them back. He touches his mother's pendant and looks at the stars. He relaxes and smiles.

EXT. BOARDING SCHOOL - YARD - DAY

Jake, Andrew, and several other children are playing catch with a football. Jake looks at JERRY, 12, a slightly retarded kid. Jerry throws the ball far away and no one catches it, but he thinks he did well.

                 JERRY
                 Yeah!

                 JAKE
          What are you doing?

Andrew interrupts Jake and makes him a signal to let him be. Jake realizes it and makes up for it.

                 JAKE
          Great play Jerry!

In the distance, Father Callahan and Father Flanagan observe Jake.

            FATHER CALLAHAN
     Tell me... What do we know about
     this new boy Jake Hallenbeck?

            FATHER FLANAGAN
     He comes from a very wealthy
     family... grandfather is very
     powerful... religious family... and

> he was giving them a lot of trouble... problem child...

FATHER CALLAHAN
Problem child? Well he's done well here... we'd have to keep an eye on him closer...

Just then, Father Rivers, from the reception, approaches Jake.

FATHER RIVERS
Jacob Hallenbeck?

Jake looks at him.

FATHER RIVERS
You've got a visitor.

INT. BOARDING SCHOOL - VISITING ROOM - DAY

Jake and Valerie are talking. They are sitting in a nice, family-type room. Jake looks very agitated, and Valerie feels sorry for him but keeps her composure.

VALERIE
Are you sleeping well? Do you have any friends? How's the food?

JAKE
Oh, the food's terrible... they give us the same thing everyday... I can't take it...

VALERIE
Well at least you're going to appreciate what we eat at the

house.

Jake doesn't answer. He just nods his head.

                  VALERIE
Well are you having a good time at least?

                    JAKE
I mean Father Callahan's cool... and so is Father O'Shea, but it's not like home... I wanna go back... I've already been here three weeks and you said...

                  VALERIE
              (interrupting)
No Jake... your grandfather would kill me if I bring you back... relax Jake...

                    JAKE
No, no please! Bring me back today!

                  VALERIE
Jake... no! Do you want me to leave!?

Jake sighs in certain anger.

INT. BOARDING SCHOOL - PRIESTS' LOUNGE - NIGHT

About eight priests are congregated around a large, round table, having coffee while they talk. Amongst those present are Father O'Shea, Father Flanagan, Father Vick, Father Rivers, and Father Harris. Father Harris is talking with father Father O'Shea.

                    FATHER HARRIS
          That is clearly wrong... God never
                 saw it that way...

                    FATHER O'SHEA
          Of course it's wrong... but until
          we have some sort of birth control
               we will still be facing
          overpopulation, poverty, misery...

                    FATHER HARRIS
          We cannot censor life! God is the
            only one who can choose who will
             come to our Earth... And birth
             control is like playing God...

Father Flanagan quietly observes the conversation.

                    FATHER O'SHEA
             But we need to update our
            convictions... in today's world
               there is no other choice...

                    FATHER HARRIS
          Well... there is always our way...
             chastity... stopping their carnal
             wishes and removing the woman from
                    their desires...

                    FATHER O'SHEA
          That is old thinking... and it will
             get you nowhere in the real
             world... if we remove the woman
             their lives... what will they end
                   up with... a man?

Father O'Shea starts to laugh slightly, making fun of Father Harris. Father Flanagan looks angry and looks at Father O'Shea with a disturbing face.

INT. JAKE'S HOUSE - VALERIE'S ROOM - NIGHT

Valerie is sitting down on her bed. She looks very excited and is dressed in a very elegant manner, as though she just came back from a dinner party.

She takes out a small jewelry box that has been gift wrapped. She opens it and sees a GOLD AND DIAMOND NECKLACE. She smiles and blushes. She tries it on in front of the mirror. She looks very pretty with it.

INT. JAKE'S HOUSE - JAKE'S ROOM - NIGHT

Charlie walks into Jake's house and turns on the lights. He looks at the room with slight melancholy; he misses his brother. He looks everywhere. He sees his brother's bass and plucks one of the strings. He sees a basketball and then the picture of his basketball team. He then looks at the poster of the universe and smiles.

INT. BOARDING SCHOOL - JAKE'S ROOM - DAY

It is early in the morning. The boys are asleep. The lights penetrates through the curtains. Just then, Sexton Taylor comes in without knocking.

              SEXTON TAYLOR
Everybody up! These are your chores

for the week!

Sexton Taylor turns on the lights and puts a list on the wall.

                    SEXTON TAYLOR
            Move it! Classes are about to
                        start!

Sexton Taylor comes out of the room. The boys slowly get up. Jake gets up with laziness and slowly walks towards the list. He looks at his name on the list. His chore is laundry.

                        JAKE
                      Laundry?

INT. BOARDING SCHOOL - LAUNDRY ROOM - NIGHT

Inside a gigantic laundry room stands Jake walking towards a gigantic stack of different color clothes. Jake starts to separate the clothes into two different stacks, one of different colors and one of whites.

He keeps moving the clothes. He throws a pair of white underwear on one of the stacks but sees something that attracts his attention. He approaches the underwear and sees a LARGE BLOOD STAIN IN THE BACK PART OF THE UNDERWEAR.

He retreats with fear and disgust. We can clearly see the blood stain.

INT. BOARDING SCHOOL - CHAPEL - DAY

It is early in the morning, Father Callahan is giving mass. Sexton Taylor and Sexton Marshall are standing next to him on the altar. Jake, Andy, Albert and several other children are present.

>   FATHER CALLAHAN
>   The Lord be with you...

>   THE CONGREGATION
>   And also with you...

>   FATHER CALLAHAN
>   May almighty God bless you, the
>   Father, and the Son, and the Holy
>   Spirit.

Father Callahan blesses the Congregation.

>   THE CONGREGATION
>   Amen...

>   FATHER CALLAHAN
>   Go in the peace of Christ...

>   THE CONGREGATION
>   Thanks be to God!

EXT. BOARDING SCHOOL - AREA OUTSIDE CHAPEL - DAY

A group of boys are standing in the yard outside the chapel. They laugh and some of them even play catch with a small ball. Jake is playing with them. Father Harris is supervising them.

Albert, who has a cast in his arm, takes the ball and throws himself on a pile of leaves that the Janitor is sweeping up and then throws the small ball away to the other kids. The Janitor gets a bit upset.

                    JANITOR
              Hey! Don't do that!

Albert laughs at him.

                    ALBERT
               (to the Janitor)
              There you go... catch...

Albert takes the ball and throws it at the pile of leaves.

                    JANITOR
            Boy you keep that up and you're
                going to clean up...

                    ALBERT
              No I'm not...

Albert kicks the pile of leaves. The Janitor gets upset and moves the rake as though he were going to hit him (although its obvious that he is not going to).

                    JANITOR
              Get out of here!

Albert runs away. Father Harris sees it and gets upset.

                    FATHER HARRIS
            What on Earth do you think you are
                        doing?

                    JANITOR

That boy was kicking...

>   FATHER HARRIS
>   (interrupting)
> You may never touch the children!
> Ever! Who do you think you are?

The Janitor is silent. He doesn't know what to say or do.

>   FATHER HARRIS
>   Come with me...

Father Harris and the Janitor, who looks very fearful, walk towards the offices. The boys look perplexed, and Albert looks at the Janitor with a face of arrogance.

INT. BOARDING SCHOOL - MESS HALL - NIGHT

The boys are having dinner. Jake, who is sitting next to Andy, looks at his plate in disgust. It is the same old meatballs and rice they always have. Jake looks at Andy, who eats like a glutton.

>   JAKE
>   How can you eat that?

>   ANDY
>   They're pretty good...

>   JAKE
>   Yeah... no kidding...

From behind, Jake feels a hand in his shoulder. He is a bit scared. He turns and sees Father O'Shea.

                    FATHER O'SHEA
            Relax... it's just me... (to Andy)
             Do you like the food Andy?

Andrew doesn't answer. He keeps eating.

                    FATHER O'SHEA
                How about you Jake?

                        JAKE
             Oh no... I'm not ending up like
             that... I'm long gone before I'm
                    look like him...

                    FATHER O'SHEA
             Well... about that... I've got a
             book you're going to like... take a
                look at it... you might like
                          this...

Father O'Shea gives Jake a book about Catholicism and priesthood. Jake laughs.

                        JAKE
                 I don't think so...

                    FATHER O'SHEA
            Never say never... see ya later...

INT. BOARDING SCHOOL - COMUNAL BATHROOMS - STALL - NIGHT

Absolute silence. Jake is sitting on the toilet seat reading the book Father O'Shea gave him, or at least, that's what it seems. As we look closer, we see that he is not actually reading the book, but is rather using it as a cover for the PORNOGRAPHIC MAGAZINE his brother gave him. Jake looks at the magazine in detail when suddenly,

A DOOR IS SHUT AND SLIGHT SCREAMS ARE HEARD IN THE DISTANCE. Jake puts the magazine away and stands up.

INT. BOARDING SCHOOL - HALLWAY - NIGHT

Jake walks through the hallway from where he hears the noise. He stops at an intersection that leads to the main entrance. At the entrance he sees Father Callahan, Sexton Taylor, Sexton Marshall, and the Janitor. The Sextons and Father Callahan are as serious as ever. Jake observes them with caution, but they don't see him.

          JANITOR
  I swear I didn't do anything,
         Father Callahan.

        FATHER CALLAHAN
  You're too late... I already told
  you... I don't ever want to see you
         around here again...

          JANITOR
  But, what am I going to do? What
        about my family?

        FATHER CALLAHAN
  That is not my problem anymore...
  what I gave you as compensation
  should suffice... And If I ever see
     you again, a lot of people who
  appreciate this house, and these

>   children, could get very upset...
>   and that is something neither you,
>   nor your family, would want. Are we
>   clear? Now, please leave.

The Janitor looks very sad and walks out. Father Callahan looks in Jake's direction. Jake gets upset and runs away.

INT. BOARDING SCHOOL - JAKE'S ROOM - NIGHT

Jake gets into his bed. He stashes the book and the dirty magazine beneath the mattress. He grabs the necklace his mother gave him and touches it. He then looks into the night sky but doesn't see any stars; the sky is completely clouded. Just them,

SEXTON TAYLOR OPENS THE DOOR WITHOUT WARNING.

Jake pretends to be sleeping. Sexton Taylor explores the room with his flashlight. He lights take for several seconds as well as his bed. He then lights other parts of the room and walks away. Jake breathes out in relief.

INT. BOARDING SCHOOL - CLASSROOM - DAY

Father Harris is giving math class to several boys, including Jake, Andy, Albert, and Jerry (the retarded boy). Jerry is standing in front of the blackboard with a piece of chalk on his hand. Father Harris is scolding Jerry. The Blackboard has several math equations on it.

>   FATHER HARRIS
>   Are you stupid or something Jerry?
>   2x is not the same as x squared.

Jerry doesn't understand what it going on. Jake is getting uncomfortable.

>   FATHER HARRIS
>   Are you stupid boy? Answer me!

Jerry wants to say something, but he is too shy. He wants to walk away. Jake is getting upset.

>   FATHER HARRIS
>   What? Did you say something? You
>   are not leaving here unless you
>   give me the answer.

Jerry looks at the blackboard but he is too perplexed. He looks at the rest of the boys trying to find the answer. Father Harris realizes it gets very upset.

>   FATHER HARRIS
>   Are you trying to cheat Jerry?

Father Harris grabs him with force and is about to strike him with his hand when Jake stands up.

>   JAKE
>   No! Don't hit him! It's not his
>   fault!

Father Harris gets upset.

>   FATHER HARRIS
>   What did you say?

Jake doesn't know what to say.

                    FATHER HARRIS
            Get out of my class now! To the
                        office!

INT. BOARDING SCHOOL - WAITING ROOM - DAY

Jake is nervously waiting outside Father
Callahan's office. After several seconds,
Father Harris comes out of Father Callahan's
office. He looks extremely angry and leaves
the area. Father Callahan walks out of his
office and looks at Jake with an intense face.
He motions for Jake to come into his office.
Jake is very nervous.

INT. BOARDING SCHOOL - FATHER CALLAHAN'S
OFFICE - DAY

Jake is sitting down in front of Father
Callahan's desk while Father Callahan is
standing behind him. Jake is terrorized.

                   FATHER CALLAHAN
            Father Harris says you challenged
                        him...

                        JAKE
                      Yes but...

                   FATHER CALLAHAN
                     (interrupting)
            I am the one who will do the
                   talking Jake...

Jake is very nervous.

                        JAKE

Sorry...

          FATHER CALLAHAN
You need learn to respect your elders Jake... your mother had already told me that was your problem...

Father Callahan puts his arm on Jake's shoulders. Jake looks forward. He's panicking.

          FATHER CALLAHAN
However, I believe that what you did today was very was brave... Christ himself was someone who always took her of the less fortunate...

Jake relaxes a bit. Father Callahan takes his hand off Jake's shoulder and walks towards his desk.

          FATHER CALLAHAN
What Father Harris did was out of line... and I really admire the fact that you protected Jerry, who can't take care of himself... not everyone would have done it...

          JAKE
Thank you...

Jake relaxes.

          FATHER CALLAHAN
And just because of that... I think you deserve better... How would you like it if we switch you to a room

> with other kids of strong
> character, like you?

Jake feels better, but he is not completely convinced.

> FATHER CALLAHAN
> You will love it there...

Father Callahan picks up his phone.

> FATHER CALLAHAN
> (into phone)
> Could you call Sexton Taylor
> please?

Sexton Taylor comes in a few seconds later.

> FATHER CALLAHAN
> Taylor please accompany our friend
> Jake to his new room... you know
> which one... and make sure he
> settles down well...

Father Callahan grabs Jake's shoulder.

> FATHER CALLAHAN
> You're going to have the time of
> your life there...

INT. BOARDING SCHOOL - SPECIAL BOYS ROOM - DAY

Jake and Sexton Taylor walk into Jake's new room. The place is empty, although there are several bunk beds and the room is a lot better, and much more spacious than the others. There are, however, no windows.

                    SEXTON TAYLOR
               Yours is the top bunk...

Sexton Taylor points at a bunk. Jake looks at it in detail.

                    SEXTON TAYLOR
               Let's go! Move it!

Jake walks to the bed and looks around. He has no place to put his suitcase.

                    SEXTON TAYLOR
               Suitcases go in the closet.

Jake looks around and flinches. He looks at the bed and realizes he has no place to put his suitcase and hide the marijuana. He looks at the mattress and sees he can't hide it there either, as the bunk bed mattress is resting on a type of grill made for furniture and the bottom of the mattress can be seen entirely, which is why he decides not to hide it there.

Jake gets nervous and touches his pants, as though he were hiding something there. Sexton Taylor looks at him.

                    SEXTON TAYLOR
               What? Is something wrong?

                    JAKE
               Can I go to the bathroom?

Sexton Taylor gets a bit upset.

                    SEXTON TAYLOR
               Move it...

INT. BOARDING SCHOOL - SPECIAL BOYS ROOM - BATHROOM - DAY

Jake puts his hand inside his pants and takes out the bag of marijuana, the pipe, and the pornographic magazine. He looks around the bathroom and hides the bag of marijuana in the back part of the toilet, where the water is flushed. He does not, however, put the magazine in there.

He looks around the bathroom looking for another place to hide the magazine. Just then, SOMEONE KNOCKS ON THE DOOR.

              SEXTON TAYLOR (O.S)
      Hurry up in there! We gotta go!

In reflex, Jake throws the magazine in the toilet and flushes it.

INT. JAKE'S HOUSE - LIVING ROOM - NIGHT

Valerie, Susy and Jen (her two girlfriends) are sitting down, chatting, drinking wine. They are dressed up and look very attractive. Valerie is wearing the necklace she opened earlier.

                  SUSY
    No! You're kidding girl! Since
                 when?

Valerie blushes and takes a sip from her glass of wine.

                VALERIE

> Well we have been going out for a couple of weeks...

                    JEN
Where did you find him? Has he been good to you?

                    SUSY
Have you already?... you know...

Valerie doesn't respond, she just laughs.

                  VALERIE
Oh no girl... he's a gentleman... who do you think gave me this?

Valerie shows the necklace to her friends. Just then, the phone rings. Valerie picks it up.

                  JAKE (O.S.)
                  (from phone)
                Hey mom!

                  VALERIE
                Jake!

INTERCUT WITH:

INT. BOARDING SCHOOL - PRIESTS' LOUNGE - NIGHT

Jake is on the phone with his mom. He looks excited.

                  JAKE
Hey mom, I've got a surprise for you!

Valerie signals to her friends for them to wait for a few seconds while she is on the phone.

> JAKE
> I've been so good I've been promoted to the room of the good kids...

> VALERIE
> That's great Jake!

> JAKE
> Can I go home now?

> VALERIE
> Relax Jake... You still need some more time... you're doing great, but...

Susy and Jen look at Valerie. They don't know who she is talking to but they think she's talking to her boyfriend and they pull her out of the conversation with Jake.

> JAKE
> You told me mom... we had a deal...

> VALERIE
> Jake... can we talk later?

> JAKE
> But...

> VALERIE
> I gotta go honey... I love you, bye...

Valerie hangs up the phone and starts talking to her friends.

INT. BOARDING SCHOOL - PRIESTS' LOUNGE - NIGHT

Jake is stunned by what happened. He hangs up and walks out of the room.

EXT. BOARDING SCHOOL - ROOF - DAY

It is still daytime, but the sun is about to set. Father O'Shea is watching the hawk inside the cage. Just then, Jake walks onto the roof and walks towards Father O'Shea.

              FATHER O'SHEA
       Jake, how are you doing?!

                  JAKE
          (a bit depressed)
               Fine...

              FATHER O'SHEA
      Something wrong Jake?

                  JAKE
   It's my mom... she doesn't care
         about me...

Jake sits down next to Father O'Shea.

              FATHER O'SHEA
   Oh Jake... I'm sorry, what makes
        you say that?

                  JAKE
   I called her and she hung up on
            me...

FATHER O'SHEA
Oh I'm sure it's okay Jake, relax... you probably caught her at the wrong time... smile Jake... Phoenix is right here, and he's fine... we're probably going to have to let him go soon.

JAKE
I'm gonna be sad to see him go...

FATHER O'SHEA
That's how it has to be... it's the circle of life...

JAKE
Yeah... I guess so... Hey, did I tell you I was switched to the brave boys room?

FATHER O'SHEA
What are you talking about?

JAKE
Don't you know about that? The boys who sit in the round table in the mess hall...

FATHER O'SHEA
Oh... I didn't know those were the brave boys...

JAKE
Yeah... I'm really excited...

INT. BOARDING SCHOOL - MESS HALL - NIGHT

The boys are walking into the mess hall. Jake and Father O'Shea walk in and walk towards their respective tables (Jake walks to the brave boys room). Andy sees that Jake is walking towards another table and catches up with him.

                    ANDY
            Where are you going?

                    JAKE
            Oh didn't I tell you? I was
                  switched...

                    ANDY
                   Where?

                    JAKE
                Over there...

Jake points towards the brave boys table. Andy seems horribly surprised.

                    ANDY
            Get the hell out of there...

                    JAKE
                 What? Why?

Sexton Taylor is walking towards them and interrupts them.

                 SEXTON TAYLOR
            Common! To your tables!

                    ANDY
                  (to Jake)
            I'll tell you later...

Jake walks away with a strange face towards his table. The Waiters start serving the food.

The boys of the new table are all quiet; nobody talks. Jake is surprised. He turns towards the other tables and sees all the other boys talking and laughing and then looks at the ones in his own table and sees that something is wrong.

Jake is served the typical meatballs and rice. The boys start eating but Jake doesn't want to. He doesn't want to eat that again.

INT. BOARDING SCHOOL - KITCHEN - NIGHT

Jake is discretely walking through a gigantic kitchen looking for something to eat. He walks quietly, as though not to make any noise. He opens a small storage been and sees dozens of bags with cookies. Jake opens one and starts eating the cookies like a glutton.

A NEARBY NOISE IS HEARD.

Jake turns in fear. He quickly grabs two more bags of cookies, puts them between his clothes and runs out of the kitchen. A few seconds later, Sexton Taylor walks into the kitchen with a flashlight in hand, looking around.

INT. BOARDING SCHOOL - HALLWAY - NIGHT

Jake quietly walks down the hallway, making sure not to make any noises. He constantly looks back. Just then, he walks next to the door to Father Callahan's office and hears the CRIES OF A BOY as well as a CONSTANT BREATHING.

Jake is terribly surprised. He approaches the door and clearly hears the crying.

He also hears someone breathing intensely. He doesn't know what it is, but he backs off.

> FATHER CALLAHAN (O.S.)
> (from inside the room)
> Do it... Christ will thank you.

The boy on the other side of the door lets go a loud cry. Jake is frightened and runs to his room.

INT. BOARDING SCHOOL - SPECIAL CHILD'S ROOM - NIGHT

Jake walks into his room, where everybody is asleep. Jake is confused, he doesn't know what's going on. He climbs on his bunked and lies down. He looks at the wall, as though he were looking for the window and the cosmos, but doesn't find anything, just the wall. The room has no windows. Jake tries to calm down.

Just then, the door to the room opens again. RICHARD, 12, walks into the room. Jake discretely looks at him and sees that he IS CRYING. The boy touches his behind as though it were hurting.

Jake is terribly confused and worried. He takes his necklace and touches the cross to find comfort.

INT. BOARDING SCHOOL - YARD - DAY

The boys are playing in the yard. Father O'Shea, Father Vick, and Father Rivers are supervising the children. Jake is not playing. He walks towards Father O'Shea.

                FATHER O'SHEA
       It's not fair, they are shut in
            here all day...

                FATHER VICK
       Yeah... I had thought about it
       too... But, what do you have in
          mind? A field trip?

Jake walks towards Father O'Shea.

                    JAKE
        I have to talk to you...

                FATHER O'SHEA
        What's going on Jake?

                    JAKE
            Alone...

Father O'Shea puts his ear next to Jake's head. Father Vick steps aside to give them space.

                FATHER O'SHEA
         Okay... tell me...

Jake tells him something. He is very stressed out.

> JAKE
> My new room is horrible... it's like everyone's a corpse... there's something wrong and Andy won't tell me... and yesterday, one of the kids got...

> FATHER O'SHEA
> (interrupting)
> Jake relax... everything's fine... You'll see, you'll be fine in a week... same thing happened with the other room, remember?

> JAKE
> It's not the same... Yesterday...

> FATHER O'SHEA
> (interrupting)
> You're gonna see... you'll adjust... Go play now... If there's anything else wrong, let me know... relax...

> JAKE
> But...

> FATHER O'SHEA
> Go Jake! Relax... you're overreacting...

> JAKE
> Yeah... I guess you're right...

Jake leaves but is not too convinced.

INT. BOARDING SCHOOL - FATHER CALLAHAN'S OFFICE - DAY

Father Callahan is looking over a large file. On top of the file lies a photograph of Jake. Just then, Jake walks into the office.

                FATHER CALLAHAN
      Jake... great to see you... Please,
                  relax...

Jake sits down. Father Callahan stands up and looks out the window, with his back turned towards Jake.

                FATHER CALLAHAN
      Tell me Jake... How are you? Tell
      me about you... Do you still miss
                your home?

                    JAKE
            Yes... I really do.

                FATHER CALLAHAN
      Who do you miss the most? Your mom?
          Your brother? Grandpa?

                    JAKE
        Well... all of them really.

                FATHER CALLAHAN
      But, I guess your mom is the one
       you miss most of all, right?

                    JAKE
             Well... yes...

                    FATHER CALLAHAN
              Would you like to have another
                    visit from her?

Jake smiles.

                    FATHER CALLAHAN
              Great... I have a proposition for
              you... I will talk to your mom to
              arrange another visit soon... the
              less you miss her, the better off
                  you'll be with us here...

                         JAKE
                    Yeah... I guess.

                    FATHER CALLAHAN
              But... don't forget what Christ,
                   our Lord, told us...

Father Callahan points at a painting of Christ on the wall.

                    FATHER CALLAHAN
              That we have to help each other...
                 I will help you, but you need to
                 understand that one day, you are
                   going to have to help me....

Jake looks at him with a strange face. Father Callahan walks towards him.

                    FATHER CALLAHAN
                     Like friends...

Father Callahan gives him a very affectionate pat on the cheek.

                    FATHER CALLAHAN
                 We are friends, aren't we?

Father Callahan puts his hand on Jake's shoulder and looks at him with intensity. Tension is absolute and total.

SOMEONE KNOCKS ON THE DOOR. In reflex, Father Callahan straightens out and takes his arm off Jake.

                    FATHER CALLAHAN
                      (irritated)
                      Who is it?

                    FATHER VICK
                    (from the door)
                 It's father Vick...

Father Callahan gets upset.

                    FATHER CALLAHAN
                      Come in...

Father Vick comes into the office and is surprised to find Jake there.

                    FATHER VICK
                 Are you busy, father?

                    FATHER CALLAHAN
                 No... Jake was just leaving...

Jake leaves. Father Callahan seems irritated and looks at Father Vick.

INT. BOARDING SCHOOL - CLASSROOM - DAY

Jake walks into a classroom. The kids sit down. Jake looks very alarmed and stressed out. He sits down next to Andrew. Father Harris is giving class. Jake tries to talk to Andy.

                  JAKE
             (whispering)
                  Hey...

Andy looks at him.

                  JAKE
     You need to tell me something
     now!... No more lies! Tell me
                  now...

                  ANDY
                  What?

                  JAKE
   You know what I'm talking about...
    What is it with the kids in my
     room? What are they hiding?

                  ANDY
              Nothing...

                  JAKE
   What? You said there was something
     weird and told me to get out of
                there...

Andy gets serious.

                  ANDY
    I can't tell you... you don't wanna
     know... trust me, just get out of

                    there now!...

                         JAKE
                    Please man...

Andy raises his voice on purpose.

                         ANDY
                         No!

Father Harris turns around as he hears Andy's voice.

                      FATHER HARRIS
                Hey, Andy! Move over here!

Father Harris points at a chair on the side of the room. Andy stands up and moves. Jake looks at him with anger.

EXT. BOARDING SCHOOL - ROOF - NIGHT

Jake is leaning on the hawk's cage. He is feeding it, talking to it, and watching the stars.

                         JAKE
             I don't know... I don't know... I
             wanna to home, I'm scared... there
                 is something weird here...

Jake looks at the hawk's wings. They are almost perfectly healed.

                         JAKE
               You are free... a few more days and
                       you're a gonner.

Jake looks at the sky and at the stars.

INT. FANCY RESTAURANT - NIGHT

Inside a minimalist, expensive type restaurant, sit Leonard Hansen, (Valerie's suitor), and Valerie (Jake's mom). They are drinking wine and are eating from the same elaborate desert. They are talking and flirting.

> VALERIE
> Oh no! My dad was a real psycho... he didn't let me do anything... he even beat one of my boyfriends up.

> LEONARD
> Well, I guess I was lucky huh? I don't like to mess with older guys...

They both laugh. She blushes and he approaches her.

> LEONARD
> Hey, I wanted to tell you... I'm going to Miami in two weeks for a business thing... I wanted to ask you if you wanted to come.

Leonard looks at her directly. Valerie takes a sip from her wine and smiles.

> VALERIE
> Oh, I'd love to.

Leonard smiles at her and takes her hand. She smiles at him, creating a certain sexual tension.

      LEONARD
  Is that okay with your kids?

      VALERIE
  Oh yeah... it's fine... it's just
    for a couple of days.

INT. BOARDING SCHOOL - SPECIAL BOYS ROOM - NIGHT

Jake walks into the special boys room, where everyone is already asleep. Jake climbs on his bunk bed and lies down. Suddenly, from the next bunk bed, ALFRED, 12, speaks to him.

      ALFRED
    (whispering)
   Ptssss... hey...

Jake looks at Alfred.

      JAKE
    What?

      ALFRED
  Did you go to your...?

Jake is surprised.

      JAKE
  Did I go to my what?

      ALFRED
  Spiritual guidance...

Jake doesn't know what to say.

> JAKE
> What?

> ALFRED
> Spiritual guidance... the favors you give father Callahan...

> JAKE
> What favors?...

> ALFRED
> These...

Alfred mimics the movement of a masturbating hand. Jake gets very upset.

> JAKE
> What?!

> ALFRED
> Yeah... when you need to help Father Callahan with his sickness...

> JAKE
> What sickness? What the hell are you talking about?!

> ALFRED
> Don't you know? What are you doing in this room if you don't know?

Jake is in shock. He is petrified with fear. He hides under the sheets. He grabs his necklace with fear.

INT. BOARDING SCHOOL - PRIEST'S LOUNGE - DAY

Jake is dialing a number on the land line. As he does, he looks at a statue of Jesus and looks around to make sure no one come in. He looks very worried.

INT. JAKE'S HOUSE - CHARLIE'S ROOM - DAY

Inside a room decorated with rock band posters, Charlie is listening to heavy metal music. The phone rings but Charlie doesn't hear it.

INT. BOARDING SCHOOL - PRIEST'S LOUNGE - DAY

Jake is getting very worried because no one is answering the phone.

                    JAKE
          Common'... pick up... pick up...

INT. JAKE'S HOUSE - CHARLIE'S ROOM - DAY

Charlie is still listening to the Heavy Metal Music. The phone continues ringing, but he doesn't hear it. Just then, he realizes the phone is ringing and answers it.

                    CHARLIE
                  Hello....

INTERCUT WITH:

INT. BOARDING SCHOOL - PRIEST'S LOUNGE - DAY

Jake is petrified with fear, talks at top speed, and constantly looks around to see if no one comes in.

>   JAKE
>   Charlie!

>   CHARLIE
> Hey Jake! What's going on man?!

>   JAKE
> Charlie you gotta help me... put
>   mom on the line...

>   CHARLIE
> She's not in man... it's just me...
>   what's going on?

>   JAKE
> There's something really weird
> here... I need you to talk to mom
> and tell her to get me outta here
>   now or they're going to...

>   CHARLIE
>   (interrupting)
> Wow, wow... Charlie, calm down...
>   what...

Jake hears how the door to the Priest's lounge is opened and has no choice but to hang up and hide beneath a table.

Sexton Taylor walks into the room and looks around as he always does. Just then, the phone rings. Sexton Taylor answer it.

>   SEXTON TAYLOR

                        Yes...

INTERCUT WITH:

INT. JAKE'S HOUSE - CHARLIE'S ROOM - DAY

Charlie is on the phone.

                       CHARLIE
             Can I speak with Jake Hallenbeck
                       please!

Sexton Taylor is very surprised.

                    SEXTON TAYLOR
                    Who's calling?

                       CHARLIE
             This is his brother Charlie... I
             really need to speak with him...

                    SEXTON TAYLOR
             I'm sorry but I'm under strict
             orders that the boys can't talk to
             anyone but their parents... so I'm
                afraid I can't help you...

                       CHARLIE
                        But...

                    SEXTON TAYLOR
                    (interrupting)
                Sorry... thank you...

Sexton Taylor hangs up the phone. He is extremely surprised. He looks around the room and then at the phone.

133

HE TEARS THE CABLE OFF THE PHONE AND WALKS OUT
OF THE ROOM.

INT. JAKE'S HOUSE - CHARLIE'S ROOM - DAY

Charlie still has the phone in his hand. He is
very surprised and doesn't know what to do?

INT. BOARDING SCHOOL - PRIEST'S LOUNGE - DAY

Jake walks out of his hiding place and looks
at the phone but sees it is no longer connected
to the wall. He starts thinking, reflecting,
and terrorizing.

>   FATHER CALLAHAN (V.O.)
>   ...one day you are going to have to
>   help me... as friends...

Jake starts to get very nervous.

>   ALFRED (V.O.)
>   ...When you need help Father
>   Callahan with his sickness...

Jake gets very nervous and starts breathing
very heavily.

>   FATHER CALLAHAN (V.O.)
>   ...do it, Christ will thank you...

Jake is almost hyperventilating.

>   JAKE
>   I'm outta here...

EXT. BOARDING SCHOOL - YARD - DAY

Jake is climbing the tree from which Albert fell so that he can escape. He climbs and climbs with all the strength and determination in the world.

INT. BOARDING SCHOOL - HALLWAY - DAY

Sexton Taylor is walking around the hallway, looking inside the classrooms, looking at the kids who are taking class. He walks for several seconds, until he walks outside the building.

EXT. BOARDING SCHOOL - YARD - DAY

Sexton Taylor walks out the building and sees the tree Jake was using to escape.

JAKE IS NOT THERE. SEXTON TAYLOR SEES THAT ONE OF THE BRANCHES FROM THE TREE IS BROKEN AND LYING ON THE GRASS.

Sexton Taylor turns deadly serious. He realizes something and starts running towards the entrance at top speed.

EXT. BOARDING SCHOOL - OUTSIDE THE WALLS OF THE SCHOOL - DAY

Jake runs at top speed through a large field. In the distance, the highway can be seen. Behind him stand the walls of the boarding school. Jake keeps running for several seconds when, from behind,

SEXTON TRAYLOR GRABS HIM FROM THE NECK AND STOPS HIM, BREAKING THE NECKLACE HIS MOTHER GAVE HIM.

Jake gets extremely nervous.

                    SEXTON TAYLOR
              What are you doing? Are you
                        escaping?

Jake doesn't know what to answer. He is terrorized. He looks at his broken necklace on the floor.

EXT. SCHOOL - SOFTBALL FIELD - DAY

Valerie and Leonard are sitting on the bleachers of a small Softball Field. Mandy, Leonard's daughter, is on home plate, about to bat. Leonard and Valerie celebrate her.

                       LEONARD
              Common' Mandy! Common'... you can
                        do it!

Valerie applauds and cheers. Leonard appears to be very nervous and puts his arms around Valerie. Valerie's cell phone rings but she doesn't answer it.

The pitcher pitches the ball and Mandy hits it with a lot of skill. The ball flies away to center field. Valerie and Leonard celebrate her with a lot passion. Valerie's cell phone vibrates again. She looks at it but chooses not to answer.

INT. JAKE'S HOUSE - CHARLIE'S ROOM - DAY

Charlie hangs up the phone. He is upset.

                    CHARLIE
                    Shit...

INT. BOARDING SCHOOL - FATHER CALLAHAN'S
OFFICE - DAY

Father Callahan is talking with Jake, he looks
very upset and Jake looks extremely fearful.

                FATHER CALLAHAN
            So let get me this straight,
            Jake... you simply decided this
            place wasn't for you, and escaped?

Jake doesn't say anything.

                FATHER CALLAHAN
            What would your mom, or better yet,
            your grandfather, think about this?

                    JAKE
            No, no, no... please don't tell
                        them.

                FATHER CALLAHAN
            Well, that depends entirely on you
            Jake... what you did here today is
            inexcusable, and an act like that
                needs suitable punishment.

Father Callahan looks at Jake right in the
eyes.

                FATHER CALLAHAN
            But I would be willing to forget it
            all if you swear to me that you
            will help me when I need your
                        help...

Jake doesn't know what to answer.

> JAKE
> Yes, yes... just don't tell my mom...

> FATHER CALLAHAN
> I won't... but only if you keep your promise... will you be my friend when I need you?

> JAKE
> Yes...

> FATHER CALLAHAN
> Great... by the way... Sexton Taylor gave me this.

Father Callahan takes out the PENDANT Jake was carrying in his neck. It is still broken.

> FATHER CALLAHAN
> It broke... but if you want we can fix it later.

Father Callahan smiles at Jake.

INT. BOARDING SCHOOL - CHAPEL - DAY

Father O'Shea is standing on the altar of the chapel, setting up for evening mass, when Jake comes in running. He looks very upset.

> JAKE
> You gotta help me now!

Father O'Shea gets a bit alarmed.

					FATHER O'SHEA
				What's going on Jake?

					JAKE
				We need to talk, now!

					FATHER O'SHEA
				About what? Tell me...

					JAKE
			Not here! Let's go upstairs... to
					the roof...

EXT. BOARDING SCHOOL - ROOF - DAY

Jake is talking to Father O'Shea.

					FATHER O'SHEA
			That can't be... there's no way
					Jake...

					JAKE
			You have to believe me! Why would I
					be lying?

					FATHER O'SHEA
			Okay... let's say it's true...

					JAKE
				It's true!

					FATHER O'SHEA
			Okay, okay it's true... what do we
					do?

					JAKE
			I don't know... I can't try to

escape again, and my mom is never going to believe me...

                FATHER O'SHEA
Well I can't talk with Father Callahan... the only person I could talk to is Father Flanagan... he knows people in the Vatican.

                JAKE
But isn't he a friend of Father Callahan? Is he going to believe us?

                FATHER O'SHEA
He has to... he might be his friend but he's not going to turn his back on something like this... and if he doesn't we'll figure it out... we gotta try... there's also the reporters... they are coming tomorrow for the second part of the interview...

                JAKE
The Reporters? How do you know that?

                FATHER O'SHEA
Father Callahan told us... but we can't tell them without proof... imagine the scandal... let's just check with Father Flanagan tonight, and we'll see tomorrow... meanwhile, you just relax... anything comes up just come get me, okay?

                    JAKE
     But what if Father Callahan finds
                    out?

              FATHER O'SHEA
     Just relax Jake... he's gonna be
        very busy tomorrow with the
                 reporters...

INT. BOARDING SCHOOL - FATHER FLANAGAN'S
OFFICE - NIGHT

Father O'Shea is talking to Father Flanagan.
Father Flanagan is very self-confident.

             FATHER FLANAGAN
     Are you sure about what you are
            saying, Father O'Shea?

              FATHER O'SHEA
     Well, I don't have proof, but we
             can't wait for...

              FATHER O'SHEA
                (interrupting)
     Well if you don't have proof you
      should be more careful with what
                  you say...

              FATHER O'SHEA
     Then what? Are you just going to
                ignore this?

             FATHER FLANAGAN
        I think the best you can do is
       remain quiet and let things take
     their course... believe me, it will
     be better for you... the person you

>   are accusing is someone who is very
>   dear to many powerful people...
>   better stay put, because the more
>   you cooperate, the faster you will
>   rise in this church.

>   FATHER O'SHEA
>   But you can't...

>   FATHER FLANAGAN
>   (interrupting)
>   This meeting... is over... go with
>   God, Father...

Father O'Shea is very upset, but has no other choice but to leave.

EXT. JAKE'S HOUSE - NIGHT

A luxurious sports vehicle pulls over outside Jake's house. Valerie and Leonard get out of the car. Valerie looks drunk. They walk towards the house.

INT. JAKE'S HOUSE - FOYER - NIGHT

Charlie is sitting down on a chair on the foyer. He looks very serious. The main entrance opens. He turns and sees Valerie and Leonard walking in, they are holding hands. They are surprised by Charlie's presence.

>   VALERIE
>   Charlie? What are you doing here?

>   LEONARD
>   Hi... you must be Charlie...

Charlie ignores him.

>   CHARLIE
> Mom, when is Jake coming back?

>   VALERIE
> Oh, I don't know Charlie... Why are
>   you asking me now?

>   CHARLIE
> Jake called me today... that he
> can't be in that hole anymore...
> You promised him that if he was
>   good he could leave...

Valerie and Leonard get upset but they try to hold it in.

>   VALERIE
> Yeah but it's not that easy
>   Charlie...

>   CHARLIE
> No, I guess not... I guess you're
>   the easy one.

Charlie stands up and leaves. Leonard looks at her awkwardly.

>   LEONARD
> I'll call you tomorrow...

>   VALERIE
> Sorry for the scene...

INY. BOARDING SCHOOL - FATHER O'SHEA'S ROOM - NIGHT

Father O'Shea is sitting on his desk, thinking about what just happened. He can't believe what has just happened and is so upset he is about to cry. His room is decorated with pictures of him and different groups of kids.

                    FATHER O'SHEA
              It can't be... it can't be...

Father O'Shea looks at the cross hanging from the wall and at the portrait of Father Callahan next to it. He is very upset.

INT. BOARDING SCHOOL - FATHER CALLAHAN'S OFFICE - NIGHT

Father Callahan is talking with Father Flanagan. They are deadly serious.

                    FATHER CALLAHAN
              We'll have to send him far away...

                    FATHER FLANAGAN
              I think that in these cases it is
              better to have to enemy close...

                    FATHER CALLAHAN
              True... but we have to keep him
                         quiet...

                    FATHER FLANAGAN
              I think I know how... but in the
              meantime, we can't have any trouble
              tomorrow... the reporters are
                         coming...

INT. BOARDING SCHOOL - HALLWAY - DAY

Father O'Shea looks at Jake as he walks towards the mess hall but stops him.

                    FATHER O'SHEA
      Jake, you were right... we are not
        going to get any help here...
      Father Flanagan is in on it too...

                        JAKE
      So what are we going to do? We have
                  to leave.

Father O'Shea looks around to make sure no one is looking at them and pulls Jake to the side.

                    FATHER O'SHEA
        We'll see if we can tell the
     reporters tomorrow. We have to make
      sure they know... this can't stay
       like this... then we are going to
        call the police and leave...

                        JAKE
    What if we just leave right now?

                    FATHER O'SHEA
     You're not the only victim here
      Jake... there are other kids
     here... the reporters need to know,
     they will look into it, and they
    are the only ones that will believe
     us... they are already publishing
      an article on them... they will
                help us...

                        JAKE
     But what if today I get...? you
                   know...

                    FATHER O'SHEA
            Don't worry... today he's busy with
              the interview... I'll talk to the
            reporters today... If I can't we'll
              call the police and we'll leave
                    tonight... deal?

                         JAKE
                       Deal...

Jake feels much better and hugs Father O'Shea.
They don't notice, but in the distance, Father
Flanagan is watching them.

EXT. BOARDING SCHOOL - FRONT YARD - DAY

It is early in the morning. Two vans park
outside the main entrance to the main
building. Father Callahan, Father Flanagan,
Sexton Marshall, and several other priests are
there waiting.

Reporter Harper, and several other reporters
and camera men get off from the van. Father
Callahan smiles at them.

                    FATHER CALLAHAN
                      Mr. Harper!

EXT. BOARDING SCHOOL - MAIN YARD - DAY

Father O'Shea is walking in direction of the
main entrance of the boarding school, towards
the reporters, when, from behind, Father
Rivers and Sexton Taylor pull him and look at
him.

                    FATHER RIVERS
           Father O'Shea... I'm so glad we ran
           into you... I need you to accompany
                    us on an errand....

Father O'Shea looks at Sexton Taylor, who is very intimidating.

                    FATHER O'SHEA
           But I need to go get the reporters.

                    FATHER RIVERS
            Don't you worry about that...
           Father Callahan is with them... we
                  need you to help us.

Father O'Shea doesn't know what to do.

                    FATHER RIVERS
            Common'... the sooner we go, the
                  sooner we come back...

Sexton Taylor subtly touches him in the shoulder as though to intimidate him but not to alarm him. Father O'Shea agrees.

                    FATHER O'SHEA
                        Okay...

Father Rivers and Sexton Taylor take him in opposite directions.

INT. BOARDING SCHOOL - MESS HALL - DAY

The Boys (Jake included) are having breakfast while Father Callahan and the reporters walk through the place. Jake nervously watches as Father Callahan talks with Mr. Harper the

Reporter. The Cameramen are taking pictures. Jake looks all around him but doesn't see Father O'Shea anywhere.

Sexton Marshall approaches Father Callahan and whispers something his ear. Father Callahan nods his head and continues talking to Mr. Harper.

INT. STORE ON THE HIGHWAY - DAY

Inside a type of antique store on the side of a desolated highway, Father Rivers, Sexton Taylor and Father O'Shea, walk through the store. They look around and stop next to a few old trunks.

                FATHER RIVERS
        This one could be a good
     purchase... wouldn't you say,
              Father O'Shea?

Father O'Shea looks at the door of the store. He looks desperate.

                FATHER O'SHEA
      Yes, they are perfect... now
                let's...

                FATHER RIVERS
             (interrupting)
      I don't know... let's keep
               looking...

Father O'Shea gets even more desperate.

INT. BOARDING SCHOOL - YARD - DAY

At the garden Jake is standing next to a couple of boys who are playing catch, but he is not playing; he is watching as how Father Callahan, Mr. Harper and several other Reporters and Priests walk next to them. Jake looks at them with impotence, he knows he has to do something.

Just then, he sees something that attracts his attention. He looks at the wall through which he escaped. The wall looks higher. He looks at it in detail and sees that in fact, IT IS MUCH TALLER.

THE WALL IS COLORED IN DIFFERENT SHADES OF THE SAME COLOR, AS THOUGH NEW BRICKS HAVE BEEN PLACED OVER TIME AND THE WALL HAS BEEN MADE HIGHER OVER TIME.

He gets even more scared. He knows he's a prisoner.

He then turns to the reporters and Mr. Harper and realizes he needs to let them know. He turns towards the main building for a second and runs towards it.

INT. BOARDING SCHOOL - YARD - DAY

Jake walks towards Father Callahan and Mr. Harper. In his hand he holds a FOLDED PIECE OF PAPER.

Father Callahan and Mr. Harper are talking when Jake runs by them and "accidentally" steps on Mr. Harper, the reporter.

JAKE

Sorry...

Jake continues running through the yard. Father Callahan and Mr. Harper look at Jake, but they don't give him much importance and continue their way. Jake looks at them. HE IS NO LONGER HOLDING THE SHEET OF PAPER.

EXT. STORE ON HIGHWAY - DAY

Sexton Taylor and Father O'Shea are loading furniture into the trunk of a large pick-up truck. Father O'Shea is drenched in sweat.

EXT. BOARDING SCHOOL - YARD - DAY

The Reporters put their equipment inside the vans. Mr. Harper greets farewell to Father Callahan and his crew.

                    HARPER
        It's been a pleasure, Father
            Callahan, thank you...

                FATHER CALLAHAN
        Oh Please, Mr. Harper... thank you
            for a job well done... I don't
        doubt the article will fit in with
            the quality standards that we
                       expect.

                    HARPER
        You can be sure of it father.

They shake hands. Harper gets into the vehicle, and they drive away until they reach the main gate of the Boarding School.

EXT. PICK UP TRUCK - ON STREET - DAY

The Pickup Truck is driving through the highway en-route to the boarding school. Father O'Shea looks very upset.

INT. BOARDING SCHOOL - HALLWAY - DAY

From a window, Jake observes as the Reporters drive away and out of the school.

EXT. BOARDING SCHOOL - FRONT YARD - DAY

Father O'Shea, Sexton Taylor, and Father Rivers arrive at the school and park just outside the entrance. Sexton Marshall walks out to greet them. Father O'Shea looks at him with worry.

                    FATHER O'SHEA
              Where are the reporters?

                    SEXTON MARSHALL
              You just missed them... they
                         left...

Father O'Shea looks at the floor with shame. Father Rivers gets off the truck and walks towards the main building. Just as he does, however, he turns back to Father O'Shea.

                    FATHER RIVERS
              Don't worry about unloading the
              furniture... we'll take it from
                         here...

Father O'Shea looks at him with impotence.

151

EXT. HARPER'S VAN - ON HIGHWAY - DAY

Harper is sitting on the co-pilot seat of the van when his cell phone rings. He puts his hand in his pocket to take out the phone, but as he does, he sees a note written with a CHILD'S HANDRWITING. Harper doesn't answer the phone and reads the letter and turns deadly serious. The letter is signed "Jake Hallenbeck and Father O'Shea".

INT. LEONARD HANSEN'S HOUSE - DINING ROOM - NIGHT

Valerie and Leonard are having a romantic dinner. They look at each other in sexual tension while Leonard pours some wine on Valerie's glass. Leonard smiles at him. She smiles back.

EXT. BOARDING SCHOOL - ROOF - NIGHT

Jake and Father O'Shea are sitting on the roof of the boarding school. Phoenix, the hawk, seems to have fully recovered.

          FATHER O'SHEA
I'm relieved you gave him the letter... I was frustrated... at least we know this is not going to stay here... whatever happens...

          JAKE
Now what? Do we leave?

          FATHER O'SHEA
We're gonna call the police... I'm going to leave an anonymous phone

call and then we'll leave without
anyone knowing... we'll go in half
an hour... stay here... I'll come
back...

                    JAKE
            Okay... perfect...

Jake realizes something.

                    JAKE
        Oh no! I can't... my grandmother's
        necklace is broken and I left it my
        room... we can't leave without
            it... what do we do?

Jake is very upset.

               FATHER O'SHEA
        Relax... it's fine... go to your
        room and get and I'll see you here
            in twenty minutes... okay?

                    JAKE
        Okay... but what about Phoenix?

They look at the Hawk it's ample health. It
relaxes them both.

               FATHER O'SHEA
        I think it's time to let him go...

                    JAKE
        Really? What if we take him with
            us? I'm gonna miss him.

               FATHER O'SHEA
        He's a free animal Jake... and he's

                    strong enough to go... would you
                    like it if they kept you here
                         against your will?

                              JAKE
                      Yeah... you're right...

Jake and Father O'Shea push the cage to the edge of the roof. Jake opens the door to the cage.

                              JAKE
                        Bye bye Phoenix!

Phoenix immediately flies out the door of the cage and flies away into the horizon. They look at him with melancholy and hug.

INT. BOARDING SCHOOL - SPECIAL BOYS ROOM - BATHROOM - NIGHT

Jake walks into his room to get his pendant when he sees Father Callahan holding the MARIJUANA BAG in his hand. All the children are standing in line, side by side, frightened to death. Sexton Marshall is present at the scene, as intimidating as can be. Jake is very surprised.

                         FATHER CALLAHAN
                   Who hid this in the bathroom?!

No one answers. Jake is stunned. Father Callahan looks at him with intensity. He thinks about running away. He looks at the door, but just then Sexton Marshall places himself between Jake and the door, so that

Jake cannot escape. Jake moves to towards the line of kids.

                    FATHER CALLAHAN
                  Who hid this?! Who!?

No one responds. Father Callahan gets very upset.

                    FATHER CALLAHAN
              I will not be ignored! This bag is
                  the root of all evils!

Jake walks in front of the kids.

                    FATHER CALLAHAN
                    Who's is it?

Father Callahan boils over. He takes of his wristwatch and stands in front of one of the kids.

                    FATHER CALLAHAN
                    Is it yours?!

Father Callahan STRIKES the kid with the watch on the cheek. Father Callahan then stands in front of another boy.

                    FATHER CALLAHAN
                    Is it yours?!

He STRIKES the boy with the watch on the cheek. Jake is about to collapse from fear.

INT. BOARDING SCHOOL - PRIEST'S LOUNGE - NIGHT

Father O'Shea is calling the police in the land phone. He has his back to the entrance of the priest's lounge.

> FATHER O'SHEA
> Hello, good evening, officer... I am calling from the School of the Order of the Lord... he have a terrible problem... the kids have been....

A HAND TAKES THE PHONE AND HANGS IT UP, TERMINATING THE CALL.

Father O'Shea turns and sees Father Flanagan and Sexton Taylor.

> FATHER O'SHEA
> Father...

> FATHER FLANAGAN
> (interrupting)
> Didn't I tell you, Father, to leave this situation be?

> FATHER O'SHEA
> But...

> FATHER FLANAGAN
> (interrupting)
> I had told you not to get involved in this... that there could be trouble... now you're the one in trobule...

> FATHER O'SHEA
> But how can you let this happen? This violates everything we are!

These are children! How can you...?

              FATHER FLANAGAN
                (interrupting)
Father Callahan has permission from the Vatican to use the children to treat his disease! The pope himself gave it to him! Do you think you are worthy enough to go against the Pope's wishes?

              FATHER O'SHEA
You are wrong Father... and you know it...

Father O'Shea tries to get out of the room, but Sexton Taylor GRABS him from the clothes and throws him towards the table with utmost force.

              FATHER FLANAGAN
            (to Sexton Taylor)
...you know what to do...

Sexton Taylor walks slowly towards Father O'Shea, who feels threatened. Father O'Shea takes a LARGE CROSS from the wall and tries to strike Sexton Taylor with it.

Sexton Taylor, however, stops the blow and strikes Father O'Shea on the head with his fist. Father O'Shea falls to the ground.

THE PHONE RINGS. Father Flanagan makes a signal to Sexton Taylor to keep the noise down. Sexton Taylor grabs Father O'Shea with easiness and shuts his mouth by force. Father Flanagan answers the phone.

                    FATHER FLANAGAN
                     (into phone)
            Hello... oh yes, there is no
            problem... it was only a stray
            dog... we've taken care of it...
            the kids were a bit scared, but
           don't worry, it's all under control
            now... thank you... we appreciate
                          it...

Father Flanagan hangs up the phone. He turns towards Sexton Taylor, makes him a signal to continue, and leaves the room.

INT. BOARDING SCHOOL - SPECIAL BOYS ROOM - NIGHT

The Boys (including Jake) are lined up, next to each other. Father Callahan is very angry.

                    FATHER CALLAHAN
               I see you don't want to
                cooperate... so once more, the
             innocent will pay for the guilty...
             one by one, you will come into my
             office and I will interrogate you
              until I find the culprit of this
                 act... I figure there's no
                        volunteers.

The Boys stay deadly silent. Father Callahan lays his eyes on Alfred, the boy who sleeps next to Jake.

                    FATHER CALLAHAN
                       You first...

Sexton Marshall pulls the boy towards Father Callahan. Jake is very disturbed and guilty.

                    JAKE
                    No!

Everyone looks at Jake.

INT. LEONARD HANSEN'S HOUSE - LIVING ROOM - NIGHT

Leonard and Valerie are passionately making out in the living room while they listen to romantic music.

INT. BOARDING SCHOOL - PRIEST'S LOUNGE - DAY

Sexton Taylor grabs Father O'Shea's neck and pushes him tightly against the wall. He can't move.

                SEXTON TAYLOR
        The less you resist, the easier it
                    will be...

Father O'Shea tries to free himself, but Sexton Taylor gives him a head butt in the face and sends him to the ground.

INT. BOARDING SCHOOL - SPECIAL BOYS ROOM - DAY

Father Callahan looks at Jake with a very intimidating face.

                FATHER CALLAHAN
                You come with me...

Jake and Father Callahan walk out of the room.

INT. LEONARD HANSEN'S HOUSE - LIVING ROOM - NIGHT

Leonard and Valerie are passionately making out to the point where sex is in plain sight. She is no longer wearing her blouse and is kissing his neck. He has unbuttoned his shirt.

INT. BOARDING SCHOOL - PRIEST'S LOUNGE - NIGHT

Sexton Taylor is mercilessly beating Father O'Shea. He kicks him several times while he is lying on the floor, picks him up and THROWS HIM AGAINST a desk. Father O'Shea, with his face soaked in blood, tries to get up, but Sexton Taylor kicks him to the ground again.

INT. BOARDING SCHOOL - FATHER CALLAHAN'S OFFICE - NIGHT

A terrorized Jake walks into Father Callahan's office. He is terrorized.

> FATHER CALLAHAN
> Sit down Jake...

Jake sits in one of the chairs in front of Father Callahan's desk. Father Callahan sits on top of the desk, right in front of him.

> FATHER CALLAHAN
> Jake, you are a problem child...
> you have tried to escape, you have
> smuggled drugs into our school...
> and this will not be tolerated...
> you need to be punished.

Jake is petrified with fear.

              FATHER CALLAHAN
But I, a charitable soul, offer you a solution, and a way out. I have helped you, and if you help me, with your own hands, I will be willing to forget everything.

Father Callahan points at his genitals. Jake doesn't know what to do. He thinks for a second, looks at Father Callahan's genitals, and PUNCHES HIM RIGHT THERE. Father Callahan screams in pain. Jake tries to escape but Father Callahan grabs him by the hair before he can leave. Jake screams.

              JAKE
              Help!

Father Callahan throws jake on the desk and pushes him, face down, towards it. He subdues him entirely. Jake tries to get free, but he simply can't.

INT. LEONARD HANSEN'S HOUSE - LIVING ROOM - NIGHT

Leonard and Valerie are almost naked and are making out completely in the couch. Sex is about to come.

INT. BOARDING SCHOOL - PRIEST'S LOUNGE - NIGHT

Sexton Taylor is mercilessly beating Father O'Shea, who is on the ground, helpless. He tries to drag himself to the door, but Sexton Taylor grabs a chair and throws it on O'Shea's back. Sexton Taylor then grabs O'Shea's head and starts banging it against the floor repeatedly.

INT. BOARDING SCHOOL - FATHER CALLAHAN'S OFFICE - NIGHT

Jake is being RAPED by Father Callahan. His head is being pushed against the desk. He is suffering completely. He tries to get free, but he can't, his eyes simply cry.

Father Callahan is amply enjoying his encounter with a sick extasy.

> FATHER CALLAHAN
> Yes... do it... Christ thanks you... Christ thanks you... Christ thanks you...

Jake looks at a picture of Christ on the wall while he feels the agony of the rape.

INT. LEONARD HANSEN'S HOUSE - NIGHT

Leonard and Valerie are having passionate sex. Valerie is moaning from the pleasure.

INT. BOARDING SCHOOL - PRIEST'S LOUNGE - NIGHT

Sexton Taylor bangs Father O'Shea's head to the wall again and again. He finally lets him go. Father O'Shea's head falls to the ground. He is completely unconscious.

INT. LEONARD HANSEN'S HOUSE - NIGHT

Leonard and Valerie reach ecstasy and cuddle together with pleasure. They are drenched in sweat.

INT. BOARDING SCHOOL - FATHER CALLAHAN'S OFFICE - NIGHT

Father Callahan reaches orgasm and lets go of Jake, who is so destroyed he simply collapses to the floor in agony.

                    FATHER CALLAHAN
          Repent yourself for offending God...

Father Callahan opens a drawer in his desk, pulls out a small jar of LIQUID MEDICINE and a XIRINGE. He puts the liquid in the syringe and injects it into his arm. He feels enormous pleasure as he does so. Jake is lying on the floor, in shock.

INT. BOARDING SCHOOL - MESS HALL - DAY

It would seem it is a normal day. The boys walk into the mess hall while the priests look over them. A very mechanical Jake, who is still in shock, walks like a disturb zombie towards his table.

Andy walks right by him as though to greet him, but he stops; he realizes what has happened and walks towards his table. Jake simply walks and sits down.

Father Callahan reaches the table and greets all the special boys.

                    FATHER CALLAHAN

> Good morning Boys... How are we
> today?

Father Callahan touches Jake's shoulder with his hand.

> FATHER CALLAHAN
> How did you sleep Jake?

Jake looks at his eyes. He wants to blow up but he simply can't, and he just nods. Father Callahan walks to the other side of the table and puts his hands on ROBERT, 12, a new boy.

> FATHER CALLAHAN
> This is Robert, your new classmate. He just got here today, give him a warm welcome and show him around...
> I'll see you all later...

Father Callahan walks away towards Father Flanagan. He whispers something in his ear. Father Callahan the immediately walks out of the room.

INT. BOARDING SCHOOL - HALLWAY - DAY

Father Callahan walks towards the priest's dormitories. He reaches a door and walks in.

INT. BOARDING SCHOOL - MESS HALL - DAY

Jake plays with his food. he doesn't eat anything. Meanwhile, Robert, the new kid, who looks very innocent is smiling. KEVIN, 12, turns towards Robert.

> KEVIN

>   And why did you come here Robert?
>
>   ROBERT
>   I had trouble with my parents...
>   but I am not going to be here for
>   long...

Robert's answer snaps out of his trance. He immediately turns towards Robert; his life makes sense again.

He looks up at the ceiling, looks at it for several seconds and then at the cross that hangs from the wall. He looks at it passionately. He is free again. He then breathes in, looks around and runs out of the mess hall.

INT. BOARDING SCHOOL - HALLWAY - DAY

Jake walks towards the Priest's dormitories. He reaches a room, but before walking into the room, he hears voices.

>   FATHER CALLAHAN (O.S.)
>   Well that would be my word against
>   yours, Father...

Jake backs off. He doesn't know what to do.

>   FATHER CALLAHAN (O.S.)
>   I don't know what makes you think
>   that your action will not have
>   consequences...
>
>   FATHER O'SHEA
>   (interrupting)
>   This will not stay like this... You

> are nothing but a tyrant and rapist who uses the name of God to justify evil... You will not get away with this...

INT. BOARDING SCHOOL - FATHER O'SHEA'S ROOM - DAY

Father Callahan, who looks physically devastated from the beating he received, is talking with a very angry Father Callahan.

> FATHER CALLAHAN
> You have no place for threats here, Father O'Shea... You have one hour to leave...

Father O'Shea looks at him with impotence.

> FATHER CALLAHAN
> And don't even think about taking the boy... he stays here... and don't even think about telling anyone about this... or what happened yesterday will be a day in paradise compared to what will happen if you disobey me...

Father Callahan leaves.

INT. BOARDING SCHOOL - HALLWAY - DAY

Jake backs off and hides. Father Callahan walks out of the room and down the hallway. Jake walks into Father O'Shea's room.

INT. BOARDING SCHOOL - FATHER O'SHEA'S ROOM - DAY

Jake opens the door to Father O'Shea's room. Father O'Shea looks at him. They both freeze for an instant. Jake runs to him with tears in his eyes. They hug and cry together.

INT. BOARDING SCHOOL - MESS HALL - DAY

Father Callahan walks into the mess hall and looks at Sexton Marshall, who immediately walks towards him.

> FATHER CALLAHAN
> Go to Father O'Shea's room and make sure he leaves...

Sexton Marshall walks away. Father Callahan sits down at his table to have breakfast.

INT. BOARDING SCHOOL - FATHER O'SHEA'S ROOM - DAY

Father O'Shea and Jake are still hugging and crying.

> FATHER O'SHEA
> We'll leave now... call the police later.

Jake wipes off his tears while he nods.

INT. BOARDING SCHOOL - HALLWAY - DAY

Sexton Marshall walks towards Father O'Shea's room and opens the door abruptly.

THE ROOM IS EMPTY.

INT. BOARDING SCHOOL - MESS HALL - DAY

Sexton Marshall walks into the mess hall and quickly walks towards the priest's table and whispers something into Father Callahan's ear. Father Callahan turns towards the special boys table and sees that Jake is not there. He is brutally alarmed and stands up with urgency.

INT. BOARDING SCHOOL - FATHER CALLAHAN'S OFFICE - DAY

Father O'Shea and Jake walk are searching Father Callahan's office. They are in brutal hurry. The open several drawers and find CAR KEYS.

          FATHER O'SHEA
        I've got them!

They both run out of the office.

INT. BOARDING SCHOOL - HALLWAY - DAY

Sexton Taylor and Sexton Marshall are running down the hallway. Father Callahan walks behind them.

          FATHER CALLAHAN
        (to Sexton Taylor)
        Hey!...

Sexton Taylor stops and turns towards him.

          FATHER CALLAHAN
  No matter what happens, don't let
  them leave! No matter what happens!

Sexton Taylor nods and Father Callahan watches as they both run in separate ways.

INT. BOARDING SCHOOL - GARAGE - DAY

Father O'Shea and Jake run into the garage and open Father Callahan's luxurious vehicle. They both get into the car. Father O'Shea tries to turn on the car, but he is so nervous he simply can't put the key into the ignition. Finally, he does and turns on the vehicle. Just then,

SEXTON TAYLOR JUMPS OUT OF NOWHERE AND OPENS THE DOOR TO THE CAR AND PULLS FATHER O'SHEA OUT.

Jake sees them struggling and gets out of the car. Sexton Taylor easily grabs Father O'Shea and subdues him.

Jake looks around the garage to see what he can use to save Father O'Shea and finds a HAMMER inside a toolbox.

Jake drops the toolbox and all the tools fall on the floor and spread around. Jake grabs the hammer and STRIKES Sexton Taylor on the back. Sexton Taylor screams and lets go of Father O'Shea, who immediately grabs a large WRENCH and hits the Sexton on the face. Sexton Taylor falls to the ground
and starts bleeding.

Jake and Father O'Shea run out of the garage. Sexton Taylor, however, regains his strength almost immediately and runs after them.

EXT. BOARDING SCHOOL - FRONT YARD - DAY

Father O'Shea and Jake run at top speed towards the main gate of the boarding school. THE GATE IS OPEN and they are quickly running for it. Suddenly, the electronic gate CLOSES.

Jake and Father O'Shea turn and see Sexton Marshall with an electric control in his hand. They start to run to the other side. Sexton Marshall runs after them.

> FATHER O'SHEA
> Let's go to the tunnels... it's the only other way out...

EXT. BOARDING SCHOOL - ENTRANCE TO THE TUNNELS - DAY

Jake and Father O'Shea quickly run to the entrance of the tunnels. They reach it and walk in. Sexton Marshall gets there a few seconds later. Before walking in, however, he hears the voice of Sexton Taylor.

> SEXTON TAYLOR
> Marshall!

Sexton Marshall turns towards Sexton Taylor.

> SEXTON MARSHALL
> Get them through the other side.

Sexton Taylor runs in another direction. Sexton Marshall runs into the tunnels.

INT. BOARDING SCHOOL - TUNNELS - DAY

Near total darkness. We are inside an old network of underground sewage tunnels half filled with water.

Jake and Father O'Shea struggle to run through the water (that is about 3 feet high). Jake constantly falls down, but Father O'Shea continues to pull him through.

              SEXTON MARSHALL (O.S.)
        There no way out! You're trapped!

Sexton Marshall is only a few dozen fee behind. He is moving at a very fast speed, but he still can't see Father O'Shea and Jake.

                  SEXTON MARSHALL
            There's no way out!

Jake and Father O'Shea are still moving, but fatigue is starting to set in, and they are losing speed and distance with Sexton Marshall.

Father O'Shea realizes what is happening and stops and looks back.

                      JAKE
                Why'd you stop?

Father O'Shea is still looking back.

                      JAKE
                  Let's go!

Father O'Shea thinks for a second and looks at Jake with absolute seriousness.

                    FATHER O'SHEA
          Jake listen to me! The third exit
          to the right is going to take you
             to a tunnel that leads to the
             highway... go through it and get
                help... I'm right behing you.

Jake doesn't know what to say. Just then,
SEXTON MARSHALL GETS THERE AND TACKLES FATHER
O'SHEA. They start to struggle. Jake takes off
immediately.

Jake runs through the tunnel constantly
looking behind him. He runs through an exit
and, after a few seconds, he reaches another
one and runs towards the third one. Just then,
as he reaches the third one,

SEXTON TAYLOR JUMPS OUT OF THE THIRD EXIT.
Jake manages to evade him but can't take the
exit and runs towards the end of the tunnels,
in the same direction he was originally
taking. Sexton Taylor turns after him.

Jake runs for a few seconds until he reaches
the edge of the tunnel. The tunnel leads to a
deep well a few feet below. Jake turns back
and sees Sexton Taylor approaching. Without
hesitating, Jake jumps into the well.

INT. BOARDING SCHOOL - TUNNELS - WELL - DAY

Jake jumps into the well. It is so deep he
sinks into it but manages to swim back up.
Sexton Taylor jumps after him. Jake tries to
run away from him. Sexton Taylor is trying not
to submerge himself, as it seems he can't
swim.

Sexton Taylor turns towards Jake, who is swimming towards the wall of the well. Sexton Taylor grabs him from his leg and sinks Jake into the well.

> JAKE
> Let me go!

Sexton Taylor uses Jake to stay afloat. Jake struggles under the water to save his life, but Sexton Taylor does not let him up.

After much struggle, Sexton Taylor grabs the wall. By the time he gets there, however,

JAKE HAS STOPPED MOVING.

Sexton Taylor realizes it and pulls Jake's body to the surface. Jake doesn't move and doesn't breathe. He looks at the body with a certain fear. Just then, from the distance, the voice of Sexton Marshall is heard.

> SEXTON MARSHALL (O.S.)
> Taylor! Taylor!

Taylor turns upwards. Sexton Marshall is standing on the edge of the tunnel, looking into the well.

> SEXTON MARSHALL
> Where's the boy?
>
> SEXTON TAYLOR
> He's dead! He drowned!

They look at each other in the eyes.

EXT. PARK - DAY

The sun is about to set. Valerie, Leonard and, Mandy (Leonard's daughter) are walking through a park. They look very harmonious. Suddenly, Valerie's phone rings. Valerie answers it.

                    VALERIE
                (into phone)
                   Hello...

We can't hear what is being said on the other line, but as Valerie listens, her face gradually turns sad and desperate. She drops the phone in shock. She starts hyperventilating and scream and crying in madness.

INT. JAKE'S HOUSE - JAKE'S ROOM - NIGHT

Charlie is lying on Jake's bed, crying like a maniac. He is devastated. He stands up, grabs Jake's cosmos poster and rips it to pieces.

                    CHARLIE
                No! No! No!

He collapses to the floor and cries uncontrollably.

INT. BUILDING - NEWSPAPER OFFICE - OFFICE OF MR. HARPER - DAY

Mr. Harper, the reporter, is sitting in his desk holding Jake's letter in his hand. He looks very intrigued and looks at his phone repeatedly. He picks up the phone and dials.

EXT. BOARDING SCHOOL - FRONT YARD - DAY

Father Callahan is standing at the main entrance of the main building of the boarding school observing as a beat-up Father O'Shea is being put in a trunk of a car by Sexton Marshall.

Father Callahan is standing next to Sexton Taylor (who has a scar on his face) and Father Flanagan.

The car takes off. Just then, Father Rivers comes out of the building.

              FATHER RIVERS
          (to Father Callahan)
      Father, you have a call.

INT. BOARDING SCHOOL - FATHER CALLAHAN'S OFFICE - DAY

Father Callahan is on the phone.

            FATHER CALLAHAN
   Mr. Harper, great to hear from you!
     How is that article coming?

INTERCUT WITH:

INT. BUILDING - NEWSPAPER OFFICE - OFFICE OF MR. HARPER - DAY

Mr. Harper is on the phone with Father Callahan.

                HARPER
    Very well, thank you... but I am

calling for a different matter.

Father Callahan feels there is something wrong.

                HARPER
I am calling to ask you about a certain Father O'Shea and a boy named Jake Hallenbeck...

Father Callahan is enormously surprised.

            FATHER CALLAHAN
Oh, Mr. Harper... I am sorry to say this but Jake Hallenbeck was in an accident and passed away... a terrible tragedy...

Mr. Harper turns pale.

            FATHER CALLAHAN
And father Callahan is no longer with us... he left for Africa to become a missionary... why are you looking for them?

Harper is stunned.

            HARPER
No... um... it's nothing... sorry...

            FATHER CALLAHAN
Really? Is there anything I need to know? Is there a problem?

            HARPER
No, no... no father...

> FATHER CALLAHAN
> I hope not Mr. Harper... I wouldn't want something to happen in the newspaper that could damage the publication of the article we are so dearly waiting for... wouldn't you say Mr. Harper?

> HARPER
> Yes, yes, of course father... there is no problem whatsoever...

> FATHER CALLAHAN
> I hope not...

Father Callahan hangs up the phone, but he is very upset. He picks up the phone again.

> FATHER CALLAHAN
> Get me Sexton Taylor please...

INT. BUILDING - NEWSPAPER OFFICE - OFFICE OF MR. HARPER - DAY

Harper is sitting at his desk. He doesn't know what to do. He is upset.

> HARPER
> Motherfucker killed them...

He picks up the phone.

> HARPER
> Mr. Martin, please...

EXT. CEMETERY - DAY

Father Callahan is speaking at Jake's funeral. Valerie is devastated, crying like a maniac. Leonard is sitting by her side, hugging her. Peter, her father, is sitting next to her.

Father Flanagan, Father Rivers, Sexton Taylor, Sexton Marshall, Jake's friends, and many other people, are congregated around Jake's small coffin. Charlie is not there.

          FATHER CALLAHAN
...and may the soul of your servant Jacob Hallenbeck, and the souls of all the faithful departed, fall under your mercy and rest in peace forever Lord... ashes to ashes, and dust to dust.

The people throw flowers on the coffin. Father Callahan then approaches Valerie and hugs her. She cries on his shoulder.

          FATHER CALLAHAN
It's always a shame when a pure, young soul, leaves us... I am terribly sorry...

          VALERIE
Thank you Father...

          FATHER CALLAHAN
And don't worry... he is watching us from up there... and he will always be in my prayers...

          VALERIE
Thank you, father...

Father Callahan takes out JAKE'S PENDANT from his jacket. IT HAS BEEN FIXED.

                FATHER CALLAHAN
      Jake was wearing this when he died.

Father Callahan gives the pendant to Valerie. Valerie cries even more and kisses Father Callahan's hand.

BLACK SCREEN:

INSERT - TITLE CARD:

"After battling with censorship for years, Alvin Harper finally published, in a European newspaper, an article denouncing Father Callahan for the rape and corruption of children in his boarding schools. Father Callahan denied all the accusations."

"Charlie Hallenbeck dedicated the rest of his life to investigate his brother's death and reveal the truth. He died a few years later under very mysterious circumstances."

"Father Callahan died a few years ago from natural causes. He was never arrested nor trialed, and dozens of cases like Jake's remain unpunished to this date."

FADE OUT.

                  THE END

Made in the USA
Columbia, SC
08 March 2024